It was just an illusion taking place in his mind. . . .

Something sharp stung his thigh. He swallowed a yelp of pain, scooted back onto dry ground, and rolled onto his side. A small creature that resembled a blue frog with a fin was attached to his leg by its teeth. It suddenly began to chomp with ravenous hunger.

The carnivorous little beast was trying to eat him! Jake grabbed the frog, yanked it off, and hurled it into the still water. Scrambling backward, Jake watched in horror as the water came alive. Thousands of Zhodran frogs rocketed into the air. They came in various shades of blue and green, and ranged in size from a couple of inches to over a foot long. The lake teemed with the creatures, and they all had snapping pointed teeth.

Jake was not going swimming.

He paused to consider the situation. The tools to accomplish the task had to be programmed into the game. Winning might be difficult, but not impossible. He just had to figure out how.

Rising to his feet, he strode boldly across the grass toward the dock.

The sentry did not react until Jake hit a strip of sand separating the grass from the water. "Halt and be assimilated," the Borg said in a flat monotone. "Resistance is futile."

Star Trek: The Next Generation

Starfleet Academy

#1 Worf's First Adventure
#2 Line of Fire
#3 Survival
#4 Capture the Flag
#5 Atlantis Station
#6 The Mystery of the Missing Crew
#7 The Secret of the Lizard People

Star Trek: Deep Space Nine

#1 The Star Ghost
#2 Stowaways
#3 Prisoners of Peace
#4 The Pet
#5 Arcade

Star Trek movie tie-in

Star Trek Generations

Available from MINSTREL Books

STAR TREK
DEEP SPACE NINE®

ARCADE

DIANA G. GALLAGHER

Interior illustrations by
Todd Cameron Hamilton

A MINSTREL®
BOOK

PUBLISHED BY POCKET BOOKS

New York   London   Toronto   Sydney   Tokyo   Singapore

to his natural liquid state. He has no patience for lawbreakers and less for Ferengi.

MAJOR KIRA NERYS—Kira was a freedom fighter in the Bajoran underground during the Cardassian occupation of Bajor. She now represents Bajoran interests aboard the station and is Sisko's first officer. Her temper is legendary.

LIEUTENANT JADZIA DAX—An old friend of Commander Sisko's, the science officer Dax is actually two joined entities known as the Trill. There is a separate consciousness—a symbiont—in the young female host's body. Sisko knew the symbiont Dax in a previous host, which was a "he."

DR. JULIAN BASHIR—Eager for adventure, Doctor Bashir graduated at the top of his class and requested a deep-space posting. His enthusiasm sometimes gets him into trouble.

MILES O'BRIEN—Formerly the Transporter Chief aboard the *U.S.S. Enterprise,* O'Brien is now Chief of Operations on Deep Space Nine.

KEIKO O'BRIEN—Keiko was a botanist on the *Enterprise,* but she moved to the station with her husband and her young daughter, Molly. Since there is little use for her botany skills on the station, she is the teacher for all of the permanent and traveling students.

QUARK—Nog's uncle and a Ferengi businessman by trade, Quark runs his own combination restaurant/casino/holosuite venue on the Promenade, the central meeting place for much of the activity on the station. Quark has his hand in every deal on board and usually manages to stay just one step ahead of the law—usually in the shape of Odo.

CHAPTER 1

"Look out, Jake!" Nog screamed. "You're targeted! She's locked on!"

Jake did not answer the frantic voice in his helmet-headset. He throttled up and urged the atmospheric fighter into a steep ascent. If this maneuver didn't work, he was dead.

"Fire, Tena Lin! Fire!" Rotor, a reptilian Selay boy, shouted encouragement to the Bajoran girl.

"I'm gonna get you this time, Jake Sisko!" Lin snarled.

Jake's onboard computer sounded an alarm as a heat-seeking missile streaked from Lin's armament pod. Jake kept his gaze on the control panel as he executed a reverse loop, leveled off, and rocketed under the enemy plane. Lin did not react in time. Her own missile streaked into her starboard engine, and the Bajoran's fighter exploded in a burst of colored light and thunder.

"Yes!" Nog's victory cry rang in Jake's ears.

"Your response time was too slow, Tena Lin," Rotor hissed. "A fighter pilot must be coiled to strike—"

"Stow it, snake-eyes," Lin snapped.

Jake ignored them. Breathless and exhilarated, he cruised blue skies at supersonic speeds, then gasped in surprise as the cockpit vanished and the world suddenly went black.

"Not funny, Nog!" Jake slipped his hands out of flexible gloves and ripped off his helmet. He turned to blast Nog for shutting down the virtual reality game before his time was up. He found himself staring at the slightly lopsided but very stern face of the Deep Space Nine's chief security officer. "Odo!"

"Classes start in five minutes, Mr. Sisko," Odo said dryly. "The IQ/Aptitudes are scheduled for today, are they not?"

"Yeah." Jake's high spirits fell.

"Then I suggest you get moving. You, too, Tena Lin."

"Right." Jake picked up his data padd, then noticed that Nog and Rotor had conveniently disappeared. He frowned, wondering why. Odo couldn't force them to go to school. Nog's father, Rom, didn't want him to go at all, so Nog only went when he felt like it. Rotor, who looked like a giant cobra with two stubby legs, was just visiting Deep Space Nine. His father was the captain of a Selay merchant ship that had put into the station for repairs.

But being Commander Benjamin Sisko's son, Jake not only had to attend, he was expected to do well.

"What seems to be the problem here?" Bokat, the Ferengi proprietor of the Games Bazaar, sauntered down the center aisle, addressing his question to Odo.

Tena Lin stomped out the door, but Jake hung back.

The constable was not happy about having another Ferengi business on the Promenade, and Bokat could not afford to antagonize him. The new arcade had opened several days before and offered a variety of games not available at Galactic Adventures, which featured holographic simulations. Bokat's inventory included replicas of historical games Jake found much more challenging. Primitive virtual reality, twentieth-century pinball, flat-screen action-adventures, and Target-Ball required physical dexterity and sharp reflexes as well as quick thinking. The carnival atmosphere of clashing sounds and flashing lights made the Games Bazaar the perfect place to get away from everyday problems.

"No problem—yet," Odo said curtly. "But if I'm forced to play truant officer very often, you'll have a big problem. Me."

Bokat shrugged. "Policing the clientele is not my responsibility."

"Galactic Adventures does not allow children to play before or during school hours." Odo scowled and leaned toward the Ferengi. "You might want to consider a similar policy."

"Sounds like bad business to me." Bokat shook his head, then met Odo's stare. "Every credit counts."

"There won't be any credits if you lose your license." Odo turned, saw Jake, and stormed forward. "School! Now!"

As Jake bolted for the door, he glanced back. Nog and Rotor were huddled under an electronic dartboard, pointing at him and laughing. Bokat was staring at him, too, but there was no hint of humor in the Ferengi's expression. Spooked by Bokat's intense interest, Jake raced out after Tena Lin.

Just before they reached the classroom, Jake grabbed Lin's sleeve and brought her to a halt. "Lin, wait a minute."

The Bajoran girl whirled on him angrily. "What is it?"

"Are you mad at me for winning Dogfight?" Jake asked. Tena Lin reminded him of the fiery Major Kira Nerys, his father's second-in-command. Both Bajorans were always ready for a fight.

"You always win that, Jake, but I can beat you on Dragon Keep. I scored over fifty-six thousand points yesterday. Set the all-time record and got a free game, too."

Lin's attitude bothered Jake. A little competitive spirit added spice to the contests, but she had become so serious about beating him, playing wasn't as much fun anymore.

"You won't get a chance to try, if Odo closes the Games Bazaar."

"Why would he do that?" Lin asked, suddenly worried.

"Bokat wasn't exactly cooperative." Engaging in shady business schemes didn't bother the Ferengi—as long as they didn't get caught. Odo always caught Nog's uncle, Quark, but it was a constant battle of wits that tried the shapeshifter's patience.

"Yeah—so?"

"So he'll use any excuse to shut Bokat down. No Ferengi will deliberately turn away paying customers, so we have to do it for him." Jake realized Lin didn't understand and explained, "I'm not going in there *before* school anymore."

Lin fixed him with a determined green-eyed gaze. "There's no law against playing before school . . . as long as we're not late. Do what you want, Jake, but I need all the practice I can get."

"They're just games, Lin!"

Lin waved him off and darted through the door.

Jake sighed. They each excelled at one type of game or another, and all four were evenly matched on the old, flat-screen action-adventures. They had won several free games recently. Curiously, Bokat had not been upset about losing the additional credits. He had seemed pleased, which didn't make sense, Jake realized uneasily. No self-respecting Ferengi liked losing money.

The bell sounded, and Jake forgot about the Games Bazaar as he trudged to his seat. He had more serious problems. His teacher, Keiko O'Brien, had arranged a conference with his father that afternoon. His Earth history term paper was overdue, and the IQ/Aptitude tests would probably show he had the intelligence of an Andorian rock-slug and wasn't suited for anything more exciting than hauling space trash.

CHAPTER 2

Jake was the last student to take the IQ/Aptitude test. However, the evaluation procedure was actually fun—more like a game than a test. Once he started, he didn't mind having to stay after everyone else had been dismissed.

A snug-fitting black helmet covered his eyes and ears so no external sight or sound could distract him. There was a prickly sensation on his scalp where the electrodes made contact, but it was easily ignored. He didn't have to write anything down or think about his answers. Images ranging from written questions to visual, situational problems flashed on the screen covering his eyes, and the device registered his responses. Observers could watch on an auxiliary screen connected to the helmet.

Jake did not know how long the test had been running. He just dealt with each new problem as it was presented.

He stood in a corridor before an open inner-airlock hatch. He heard the hiss a second before the outer hatch blew out and mentally slammed his hand on the seal-

7

control. The inner door closed before sudden decompression sucked him into space.

Who invented duotronic computer technology? When?
Dr. Richard Daystrom in 2243. *Easy.* Jake thought.
How are you feeling?
Great.
Instantly the view shifted to show perfectly spaced, crisscrossing lines in space. *Identify.*
A Tholian Web.
Then Jake was standing in a cargo bay with red-alert

klaxons blaring. The com-panel showed that the inertial dampeners and all backup systems would fail. The ship could not brake. *Result?*

Squashed against the bulkhead by the ship's forward velocity. It was not a funny situation, but the mental picture of being shot across the hold and flattened against the wall made Jake smile.

47.90 is the atomic weight of . . . ?

Titanium.

The screen darkened and the words *Test Over* blinked. Jake exhaled, relieved and exhausted, yet feeling oddly thrilled, too.

"Excellent, Jake!" Keiko removed the helmet and set it aside. "You scored an 857."

"Is that good?" Jake squinted as his eyes adjusted to standard station light.

"Very good," said a familiar deep voice.

"Dad!" Jake gasped. His father had watched the whole test.

Benjamin Sisko watched Jake now. "In fact, this test proves something we've suspected all along, Jake. You're extremely bright, and you're not working up to your potential or abilities."

Jake didn't say anything. He couldn't argue results arrived at through Federation technology. He had been betrayed by his own brain, and knowing he was much smarter than an Andorian rock-slug didn't help. Now his father would expect even more of him.

"I wouldn't worry too much, Commander Sisko," Keiko said. "Jake just needs time to find his own niche.

When he discovers a subject that really interests him, he'll apply himself."

"Perhaps, but I don't want him to lose too much ground while we're waiting. If he spent half as much time working as he does playing arcade games, that overdue term paper might be finished." Sisko turned back to Jake. "Don't you agree?"

"Yeah." Jake sighed. He knew what was coming next.

"Well, since you can't seem to organize your time and set your priorities properly, I will. No more game playing until that paper is finished—correctly—and turned in."

"Yes, sir."

"Good." Commander Sisko paused to grip Jake's shoulder on his way out the door. "I'll see you at dinner."

Keiko's words of praise fell on deaf ears as Jake left the school. Despondent, he shuffled toward the nearest crossover bridge connecting the Promenade to the Habitat Ring. He was in no hurry to get home and decided to walk instead of riding the turbolift.

At least he wouldn't have to explain being grounded to his friends until tomorrow. They were all at the Games Bazaar having fun, while he was stuck writing a paper on a bunch of crazy knights who had fought a stupid religious war on Earth over a thousand years ago. Boring.

"Pssst!"

Jake stopped dead halfway through the crossover. No one was in sight, but he suddenly felt very alone and vulnerable. Anyone could be lurking in the empty passageway. The station teemed with rowdy, merchant crewmen, aliens with mysterious codes of conduct, Klingons and Cardassians, and Bajoran political activists. Deep Space Nine could be a dangerous place for the unwary.

"Pssssst!"

"Who's there?" Jake backed up a step.

A Ferengi hand beckoned him from the open hatch at the end of the corridor. "Jake! Over here. It's me. Bokat."

Annoyed, Jake walked forward. "What is it, Bokat?"

The Ferengi grinned and rubbed his hands together. "I've got a proposition for you, Jake. A once-in-a-lifetime offer."

"Uh-huh. Like what?" Jake waited, intrigued and suspicious.

"A chance to try the ultimate game, the Zhodran Crystal Quest. Not a game for the average player, mind you. Oh, no." Bokat lowered his voice. "A game only the best dare attempt!"

"Why me?" Curiosity overcame Jake's reservations.

"Your skill is exceptional. I simply must give you an opportunity to try the impossible."

"Sorry, Bokat. I can't."

"But it's free!" The Ferengi's eyes widened in near-panic.

"Free?" Jake started, suddenly nervous. "How come?"

Bokat blinked, his mind racing. "As a reward, my boy. Uh, in keeping with the fifty-first Rule of Acquisition."

"Which is?"

"Reward anyone who adds to your profits so they will continue to do so." Bokat smiled and draped his arm

11

over Jake's shoulders. "Do you have any idea how many adults are coming into the Games Bazaar to try and top your scores?"

Jake shrugged. "No."

"A lot. They can't transfer their credits fast enough. So I must repay you. It's only right."

Jake scowled, remembering the hard look Bokat had given him that morning. There was no right or wrong in Ferengi culture—only profit and loss—and they were always looking for a sucker.

"Look, I appreciate the offer, but I can't right now. I've really gotta go." Jake tried to edge past the Ferengi, but Bokat's arm whipped out to block his way.

"Yes, of course." Bokat's calculating frown sent a shiver up Jake's spine. "It's an open invitation. Anytime. However"—Bokat leaned forward, pressing Jake against the bulkhead—"this is our secret. No one else must know. Understand?"

Jake looked into narrowed, Ferengi eyes and nodded quickly. "No. I won't say anything. Promise."

"Such an intelligent young person. For a human. I can't have people thinking I'm an easy touch. It would ruin my reputation." Bokat turned to leave, then looked back with a sly grin. "No one has ever won the Zhodran Crystal Quest, Jake."

Alone again, Jake sagged with relief. The thought of playing and beating a game no one else had won was an irresistible challenge . . . except for Bokat. Somehow, the Ferengi would profit if Jake played the Zhodran Crystal Quest and won.

On the other hand, he had nothing to lose by trying—

except game privileges for the rest of his life, if he didn't get the history paper handed in soon.

Jake hurried toward home with a new sense of purpose. Most of his research was done. All he had to do was organize his notes and write the paper. Once the assignment was finished, his father would let him play again, and Bokat had said he could try the impossible game anytime.

Jake raced through the turbolift doors. He had overslept after staying up late working on the paper, and he still wasn't done! Bokat's game, the Zhodran Crystal Quest, was to blame. He couldn't help but wonder why it was so difficult. He'd probably never find out. Bokat could not be trusted, and the Crusades report would take another two days to complete—longer if he couldn't keep his mind on the project.

A maintenance-access hatch by the Promenade airlock had been left open. Jake skidded to a halt. Deep Space Nine had been in ruins when Bajor and Starfleet had taken possession after the Cardassians evacuated. Miles O'Brien, Keiko's husband and chief of operations, had worked hard to get all systems functioning up to Federation standards. Leaving a hatch ajar was not serious negligence, but O'Brien was a stickler for such details. Jake decided to close it and save someone from a loud O'Brien lecture.

As he reached to hit the control panel, Jake inhaled sharply. Tena Lin was lying unconscious inside the tube with severe burns on her face and arms.

CHAPTER 3

Stunned, Jake hesitated only a second. Yelling for Dr. Bashir, he plunged into the Promenade and ran toward the Infirmary. Odo intercepted him.

"What's all the racket about, Mr. Sisko?"

"It's Tena Lin." Jake grabbed Odo's sleeve and pulled him toward the crossover bridge. "She's been hurt. Really bad."

"Where?" Young Julian Bashir, the Federation doctor on DS9, dashed across the deck to join them, carrying a medikit.

"In here." Jake shoved Dr. Bashir into the airlock. Odo stayed behind to discourage a crowd of curious onlookers.

Hanging back as the doctor scanned Lin's still body, Jake wondered why she had been poking around in a maintenance tube. He studied the interior with a mounting sense of disquiet. The tube was crammed with wires and pipes, relays and junctions, but he didn't see any signs of fire or broken electrical conduits. The burns could not have happened at this location. She must have dragged herself here after being hurt somewhere else in the tube.

Odo reached the same conclusions within seconds of arriving on the scene. "Did you see anything, Jake? Hear anyone?"

"No, nothing . . . except the open hatch."

"We'd better get her to the Infirmary," Dr. Bashir said gravely. "I can take care of the burns easily enough, but I'm worried about the coma. She's not responding to any stimulants."

Dr. Bashir lifted the frail girl, and Odo paused to look pointedly at Jake before following him to the Infirmary. "You might as well go on to school. There's nothing more you can do for Tena Lin now. I may want to talk to you later, though."

Disturbed by the accident, Jake couldn't concentrate in class. Tena Lin's parents had worked as cargo handlers during the Cardassian occupation and had stayed when the Federation took over. Any kid who grew up in space, whether on a starship or a space station, quickly learned the ins and outs of living in a technological environment. Too many mistakes were potentially deadly. Accidents happened, but Lin was too smart to have done anything as dumb as fooling around with faulty power equipment. She would have reported a malfunction immediately, even if it meant getting into trouble for playing in a restricted area.

As the day wore on, Jake's patience wore out. By the time Keiko let everyone go, he was certain Lin had met with foul play. His suspicions were supported when he rushed into the Infirmary and overheard a conversation between Odo and Dr. Bashir.

"I spoke to her parents," Dr. Bashir said. "Lin was fine when they left for work this morning. That was two hours before Jake discovered her, and no one saw her during that time."

A frown wrinkle ruptured on Odo's smooth forehead. The shapeshifter occasionally tried to refine his facial expressions, often with comical results. "Chief O'Brien hasn't found any broken power lines or short circuits in that maintenance tube or the connecting conduits, either. Could she have gotten into that hatch from another location by herself?"

"With such severe burns? Possibly, but not very likely."

"Then someone put her there!" Odo's beady eyes glittered.

Dr. Bashir was appalled. "She's just a child! Why would anyone want to hurt—" He stopped speaking when he noticed Jake standing in the entrance. "Jake. Here to see your friend?"

"Yes, if it's all right. Is she any better?"

"I'm afraid not." Dr. Bashir walked with him to the side of Lin's biobed. "Do you know her well?"

"Pretty well." Jake looked at Lin's pale face. The burns were healed, but she was still unconscious. The lights on the display above the biobed blinked and beeped, monitoring her condition. Jake wished there was something he could do to help.

"Emergency! Emergency!" A harsh, bass voice

boomed from the Promenade. "Out of my way, you miserable deck-rat!"

Odo, Dr. Bashir, and Jake turned as a tall, muscular Selay kicked an unsuspecting Nork away from the Infirmary door. The blue-furred, six-legged creature squealed and scurried up the wall. Chief O'Brien stopped to gently coax the alien down, while the giant adult cobra rushed inside carrying a limp Selay child.

"Doctor! My son—I think he's dying!"

Rotor! Jake gasped.

"Put him over here." Dr. Bashir hurried to the empty biobed beside Tena Lin and reached for a tricorder. "And you are?"

"Captain Gaynor of the Selay merchant vessel *Erlan.*"

"What happened to him?" Dr. Bashir asked, frowning as he scanned the unconscious reptilian boy.

"We're not sure, Julian," Chief O'Brien said. "I found him at the bottom of an unused turboshaft near Cargo Bay Six."

"Um-hmm." Dr. Bashir set the tricorder aside.

"Is he going to be all right?" Gaynor asked anxiously.

"He's got a fractured leg. I can have that fixed in no time, but—" Dr. Bashir paused thoughtfully. "Had he been gone long?"

Gaynor shrugged. "An hour. No more than two. Why?"

"Because he's in a coma, and there's no medical reason for it—none that I can find anyway." Stumped, Dr. Bashir shook his head. "Shock from the fall, maybe. . . ."

As Jake listened, fear tightened his stomach. Dr.

Bashir had graduated at the top of his Starfleet Academy medical class. He was a great doctor. But he couldn't cure the mysterious comas if he didn't know what had caused them.

Odo moved closer, his interest aroused. "Is the boy's coma similar to the one affecting the Bajoran girl, Doctor?"

"Quite similar actually." Dr. Bashir paused thoughtfully. "They're both in comas for no discernible reason."

"What Bajoran girl?" Gaynor demanded.

Odo ignored the question and asked one of his own. "Do you have any enemies on Deep Space Nine, Captain?"

"Are there Anticans on this station?" Gaynor bellowed with an ominous rattling sound. "I don't smell them!"

"Not that I know of," O'Brien answered, suppressing a grin.

If the circumstances hadn't been so serious, Jake would have laughed, too. He'd heard O'Brien's famous story, "The Delegate Dinner." The *Enterprise* had once transported Selay and Antican delegations to the neutral planet Parliament. Both species had applied for membership in the Federation, and it was hoped they would settle a long-standing dispute. Both groups were temporarily denied membership due to continuing hostilities. The Anticans had killed and eaten two members of the Selay party.

"Perhaps that obnoxious Ferengi, Nog, had something to do with my son's accident," Gaynor hissed menacingly.

"Nog likes Rotor!" Jake quickly rose to Nog's defense.

"I did see the two of them together yesterday," Odo observed. "However, although Nog may be too rambunctious and mischievous for his own good and my peace of mind, he's not malicious or violent."

Jake glanced at Odo, eyebrows raised. The chief of security followed a rigid personal code of justice. Still, it seemed strange to have him take Nog's side.

"Nog wasn't involved," Dr. Bashir said. "He's been busing tables for Quark all day." He walked away from the biobed, then back again. "It could be a virus—something so small or alien the sensors can't detect it. Or a bacteria. Hard to say."

"I rather doubt that, Doctor." O'Brien had installed Federation biodetectors in all the docking airlocks. "It would have to be subatomic to elude the biosensors."

"I'm going to quarantine both of them anyway. As a precaution," Dr. Bashir added quickly. "If it is a virus, it's not transmitted by air or we'd have more cases." Shooing everyone away from the immediate area, Bashir confined the two children in personal containment fields.

"That's one theory," Odo muttered.

"You have another?" Gaynor rattled and turned on Odo with a venomous hiss. His colorful cobra hood flared.

"Not exactly." Odo was not intimidated by the Selay's reptilian display of antagonism. "I have a puzzle with a lot of missing pieces, and I'm suspicious by nature. Could be a coincidence. Two accidents. Two comas. Then again—"

Jake froze as Odo turned his penetrating gaze on him. "What? Don't look at me! I didn't do anything!"

"I didn't say you did. However, you know both victims."

"Every kid on the station knows every other kid, Odo. Even the visitors. There aren't that many of us!"

"I'm aware of that, Mr. Sisko." Odo clasped his hands behind his back. "And you'd tell me anything you knew that might be relevant to the case, right?"

"Right!" Jake swallowed nervously, wondering if he had suddenly become a suspect. "But I don't *know* anything."

"Maybe you just don't know . . . what you know. Hmmm?" Odo walked out, leaving Jake stunned and speechless.

O'Brien chuckled. "Better not skip town, Jake." As he started to exit, Dr. Bashir called him back.

"I'm afraid I'll have to detain you and the Captain, Miles. You both touched Rotor. I have to make sure you're not infected or carriers . . . if there's anything to carry."

O'Brien groaned. Gaynor hissed. Jake hadn't touched either Lin or Rotor and got out of there fast.

Back in his room Jake tossed the data padd on his desk and flopped on the bed with a heavy sigh. He couldn't stop thinking about Odo's last words. But hard as he tried, he couldn't figure out what he might know that he didn't *know* he knew.

CHAPTER 4

Jake's thoughts zigzagged through a maze of troublesome questions. Had Dr. Bashir found the cause of the comas yet? Would Bokat keep his word and let him play the Zhodran Crystal Quest? What kind of game was it? How come it was so hard to win? And why was he thinking about a game when two of his friends were critically ill in the Infirmary?

Off course—again! Shaking his head, Jake focused on his computer. The paper would be finished by tomorrow, even if it took all night. *Which it might,* he thought, scanning his notes with bored detachment. Ancient Earth history had no practical value for a twenty-fourth century teenager living in a space station on the threshold of the Gamma Quadrant frontier. *Crusades* was just another name for war.

European monarchs had waged three campaigns against a distant, Mediterranean people who had different religious beliefs. They had also lived in the city of Jerusalem, which had symbolic significance in the European religion. The First Crusade conquered the city. The

Second Crusade hadn't accomplished anything. And the Third Crusade, launched to take Jerusalem back from the Kurd, Saladin, had ended in a truce in A.D. 1192. Saladin kept the city, and the Europeans were granted permission to visit.

So why, Jake wondered, hadn't they tried to negotiate a mutually satisfactory agreement in the first place! At least the Cardassians had invaded Bajor to steal the planet's natural resources. That wasn't right, but it made more sense than fighting over territory just because an important person had lived and died there twelve hundred years *before* the Crusades!

Of course, certain religious factions on Bajor wanted Starfleet to leave because they believed the Prophets' Celestial Temple existed in the wormhole. His father had proved that the revered orbs were only messages sent by the wormhole's alien creators, but facts hadn't changed the Bajorans' spiritual beliefs. However, the Federation respected Bajoran rights. Starfleet would leave the station and the wormhole rather than fight over them. Fortunately, other political groups on the planet recognized that a Starfleet presence kept the Cardassians from trying to conquer Bajor again, and a truce had been declared.

Which made his father kind of like King Richard the Lion-Hearted of the Third Crusade. Jake sat back, intrigued by the similarity between two situations that were twelve hundred temporal years and thousands of light-years apart. Maybe some aspects of sentient nature never changed—only the beings, the places, and times.

The door chimed. "Come!" Jake shouted.

"Jake! Jake!" Nog scurried into the room, ears twitching and eyes wide with excitement. "Wait'll you hear this!"

"What?" Jake turned, welcoming the diversion. "You're acting like a Ferengi who just made the deal of the century."

"Perhaps I have." Panting, Nog sat on the edge of the bed, then immediately bounced to his feet and began to pace. "This could be big, Jake. I mean, really *big!*"

"What could?" Jake leaned forward eagerly. Nog's moneymaking scams and mischievous pranks usually got him into trouble, but they also provided some thrilling moments that broke the monotony of normal routine. Life with Nog was never dull.

"I'm not supposed to say." Nog paced, wringing his hands.

"Then don't." Jake shrugged, pretending not to care.

"I did give my word." Perching on the bed again, Nog sagged and cocked his head. "Of course, everyone knows a Ferengi's word isn't worth anything."

Jake nodded. "This is true."

"Not unless the stakes depend on it." Nog bobbed his head thoughtfully. "Which—in this case—they don't. In fact, I'm not sure there's any profit in this for *me* at all."

"Then I don't see the problem." Jake smiled. "You're going to tell me anyway. So why waste time?"

"A good point." A wide toothy grin split Nog's face as he popped off the bed and hunched over, a Ferengi posture of conspiracy. "Bokat has made me an offer I can't refuse."

"Bokat?" Jake frowned, but Nog was too excited to notice.

"He has this game—nobody's ever won it. It's called the Zhodran Crystal Quest, and Bokat is going to let me try it because I'm such a good player! He thinks he owes me for making the arcade a success! Can you believe that?"

"Actually, yes, but—"

"But what? Playing won't cost me anything! It's free! I've got nothing to lose, and like Uncle Quark says, 'There's a sucker born every minute.'"

"Yeah, and you're it," Jake said.

The sparkle in Nog's eyes faded suddenly. "What's that supposed to mean, Jake Sisko?"

Jake chose his words carefully. "Bokat offered to let me play the Zhodran Crystal Quest, too, and—"

"He did not!" Nog interrupted, furious.

"Yes, he did," Jake insisted. Nog didn't want to believe that Bokat's offer was not exclusive. Jake had liked being singled out as the best player on the Promenade, too, but he was sure that Bokat had ulterior motives. "I think it's very suspicious, Nog. No Ferengi gives something for nothing."

"The fifty-first Rule of Acquisition—"

"I've heard it." Rising, Jake glared at Nog. "Did you ask for a reward or threaten to stop going to the Games Bazaar?"

"No . . ." Nog scowled.

"Me, neither. If people are going to the Games Bazaar to beat our high scores, that wasn't going to change. Bokat didn't *have* to offer us anything to keep us playing. He wants us to try the Zhodran Crystal Quest for other reasons."

"So what? He'll let us play for nothing. The thirty-seventh Rule of Acquisition states quite clearly: 'If it's free, take it and worry about hidden costs later.'"

"That's just it, Nog!" Jake threw up his arms. "What hidden costs? Why is this game so hard to win? What does Bokat hope to gain? Why won't he let everyone try it? There's something strange about this whole thing." Nog wasn't convinced, and Jake tried a different tactic.

"Did you know that Tena Lin and Rotor are both in comas that Dr. Bashir can't explain?"

"So? What does that have to do with Bokat's game?"

"Nothing, but I wouldn't enjoy playing games knowing that two of my best friends were unconscious in the Infirmary." Nog's chin jutted out stubbornly, and Jake sighed helplessly. "Just take my advice, Nog, and don't play."

"I know what you're up to, Jake. You're trying to talk me out of it because Bokat didn't really offer to let you play. You're jealous!" Spinning around, Nog stalked toward the door.

Jake hurried after him. "Come on, Nog. You know me better than that."

"Okay. Prove it. Come down to the Games Bazaar with me. We'll both give the Zhodran Crystal Quest a shot."

"Can't. I'm grounded until I get my term paper finished."

"How convenient." Huffing with indignation, Nog left.

Worried, Jake went back to his desk. Time dragged. His father called to say he'd be late. Jake ate a replicated sandwich for dinner, then took a shower, hoping to stimulate his stalled brain. He started a first draft of the paper, but repeatedly caught himself staring off into space. He couldn't concentrate or shake the feeling that Nog was headed for big trouble. That wouldn't be anything new, but this time the trouble might be more than his Ferengi friend had bargained for.

Finally, since he wasn't making any progress on the paper anyway, Jake decided to take a break. He wasn't going to get anything done until he knew Nog was all right. Anxiously he headed for the door. His father had said he couldn't *play* any games. He wasn't going to play. He was just going to watch.

Except the Games Bazaar was closed.

Jake stood outside the darkened arcade, staring through the transparent door. The overhead lamps had been dimmed, and the flashing lights on machines and screens gave the deserted interior an eerie look. Neither Nog nor Bokat was visible. Jake couldn't think of *any* reason a greedy Ferengi merchant would close down during the busiest hours of the day—except Odo. Maybe the security officer had revoked Bokat's operating license.

Too bad, Jake thought. No doubt, Nog was upset because he couldn't play the Zhodran Crystal Quest, but maybe he wasn't mad anymore. The little Ferengi had probably gone to one of their secret hiding places to pout. As Jake turned to leave, a pair of Jorsian bulls paused to peer in the window.

"Closed!" the largest bull roared. His massive partner shrugged, then both charged on to find entertainment elsewhere. Jake flattened himself against the door to keep from being trampled, then yelped in surprise when the door slid open behind him. He stumbled backward and fell inside, landing on the floor with a painful thud.

A bloodcurdling scream broke the silence.

Nog!

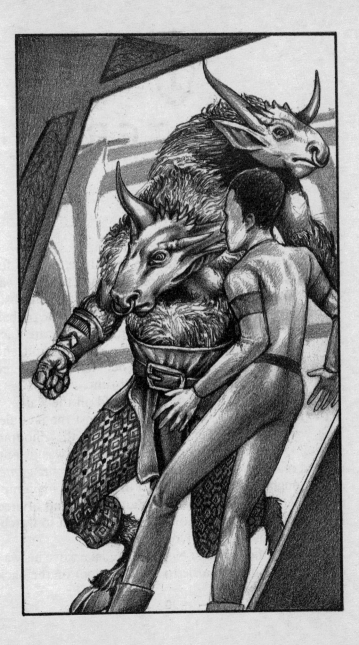

CHAPTER 5

Jake rolled under Star Raiders and froze. Except for the gongs, beeps, and whistles of the games, the shop was quiet. Nothing moved but the flashing lights. Cautiously he crept toward the back of the arcade, using the pinball machines as cover. Pausing by the antique Road Race 2000 module, he peered through the open cockpit and thought about going for help. Then he remembered Nog's terrified shriek. There wasn't time.

"Yes!" Nog's triumphant call echoed off the walls.

Feeling like a fool, Jake slumped against the module. Nog was *not* in danger. He was playing the Zhodran Crystal Quest in another room. The scream was just an excited reaction to the game. *Must be a dynamite game,* Jake thought as he stood up and brushed off his jumpsuit. Since he was already inside and Bokat had invited him, he saw no harm in joining the fun—just to watch.

"Almost gotcha. . . ." Nog laughed.

Following the sound of Nog's voice, Jake wove his way through the cluttered aisle to a sliding door on the back wall. Another panicked scream split the quiet as the door *whooshed* open. Startled, Jake hesitated just inside. The door closed behind him.

The small, dimly lit room was empty except for two chairs and some high-tech video equipment. An ornate silver headpiece engraved with unfamiliar symbols lay on the floor. A long cable connected the device to a data-chip recorder. The monitor blanked, whirred, then displayed a visual of mountainous terrain. Fascinated, Jake sat down to watch.

The view panned upward from the base of a high, rocky mound. A gold ball, resting in a shallow depression at the top of the mound, gleamed in the sun.

"Yes!" Nog's voice!

Jake laughed aloud. He was watching the scene through Nog's eyes. Clawed Ferengi hands appeared as Nog climbed toward the golden prize. "Almost gotcha. . . ." Nog reached to grab the ball.

Like Nog, Jake did not see the danger until it was too late. The rock to the left moved. Not rock. Jake shuddered. A snake. The triangular pattern on the huge viper's skin was shaded in muted greens and browns, providing perfect camouflage in the moss-covered rock. The snake struck, sinking long, sharp fangs into the Ferengi boy's leg. Nog screamed, then collapsed.

Jake blinked in confusion. The gold ball was not a crystal, but this had to be a recording of Nog's attempt to play the Zhodran Crystal Quest. Obviously, Nog hadn't won, either.

So where was he? Jake grinned. Nog was probably

31

making himself scarce because he didn't want to admit he had lost.

The monitor blanked and whirred, then started the sequence over again. The recorder was locked in Replay mode, but it was standard Federation issue. Releasing the memory lock, Jake keyed the data chip to play from the beginning. Blank screen.

A low hum sounded from the headpiece lying on the floor. Jake picked up the scrolled hardware and turned it over in his hands. His skin tingled in response to the current flowing through the heavy metal. The device was alien, but it apparently worked on the same principles as the IQ/Aptitude helmet. The player experienced the game scenarios as though they were real, and the results could be monitored on an auxiliary screen.

Another scream. This one from Tena Lin. Jake looked at the monitor and saw nothing but a wall of searing flame.

Blank screen again. Then Jake saw Selay hands clutching a rope and heard a terrified hiss. The angle switched to a view of a deep chasm below, and the image blurred as the rockface suddenly streamed past. Rotor had lost his grip. He fell into the dark pit with a squeal that ended abruptly. The screen blanked again.

"Your turn." A low, gravelly voice said from behind.

Jake jumped up and spun to face Bokat. He had been so engrossed in the monitor, he had not heard the door open and close. His own voice shook slightly when he spoke, from guilt because Bokat had caught him snooping—and dread. "I told you, I can't play. My father—"

"Your father isn't here," Bokat snarled.

Alarmed, Jake stepped to the side and reached for his comm badge—which wasn't on his chest. Oh, no! He hadn't switched it to the clean jumpsuit after his shower because he hadn't planned on going anywhere. "Where's Nog?"

Bokat blocked his access to the door. "Lost—like your other friends. But then, they weren't the best. You are, Jake Sisko."

"Lost? I don't understand." Still clutching the headpiece, Jake moved casually back the other way. He understood too well, but he wanted to distract Bokat. Nog, like Tena Lin and Rotor, had been injured playing the game. He wondered if Nog's comatose body had been found yet, and if Odo would connect the faked accidents to the arcade when it was. Not likely.

"They're lost in the game, Jake. Their physical injuries can be healed, but their minds are trapped for all eternity because they failed. You might win."

"Maybe." Jake shrugged and glanced at the headpiece. If the Ferengi kept talking, he might let down his guard long enough for Jake to rush the door.

"You must win. It's the only way you'll survive the Zhodran Crystal Quest." Bokat eased forward. "And it's the only way I'll find the Da-hahn Crystal."

"What's that?" Jake asked.

"The key to universal power." A sheen of sweat glistened on Bokat's face, and he licked his lips in anticipation. "The Da-hahn Crystal is an ancient Zhodran artifact that bestows absolute invincibility and immortality on whoever possesses it. *I* intend to have it, and you're going to help me."

Jake nodded, appearing to consider the Ferengi's proposition. The consequences of playing the Zhodran Crystal Quest were more terrible than he had imagined. Injuries inflicted by the game were real, and worse—the sinister device imprisoned the mind.

"What if I won't play?" Jake asked with cocky stubbornness. He tossed the headpiece in the air, noting Bokat's horrified expression and extreme relief when he caught it again.

"Oh, you'll play. You don't have a choice."

Jake backed up as Bokat slowly advanced. The Ferengi were small, but very powerful for their size. He was no match for the wiry merchant in hand-to-hand combat. He'd have to think his way out of this predicament.

"I don't like to lose," Bokat said. "If you win the game, I'll get the crystal and with it, the power to protect myself. If you lose, you'll be caught in the game matrix, where you won't be able to tell anyone what you know. Either way, I win."

"What's in it for me?" Jake asked, angling his backward path to avoid getting trapped against the wall. Escape was his only hope of saving himself and his friends.

"Your life and the satisfaction of winning . . . if you win," Bokat replied with a smug grin. "If you don't—"

"Not good enough, Bokat." Holding the headpiece high in the air, Jake bluffed. He didn't dare let the device break. Any chance to free the minds captured in its circuits might be lost if the game was destroyed. But

Bokat needed the game, too. Being Ferengi, he didn't understand a human's high regard for the welfare of others. Jake gambled that Bokat would believe he'd damage the device rather than play against his will. It worked.

"Be careful!" Bokat lunged for the device.

Jake ducked and bolted with the headpiece firmly in hand. As the connector tore free of the recorder, the cable whipped against his legs and lashed Bokat's arm. The Ferengi howled and hesitated, and Jake gained a few seconds. He darted from the room, tripped on the dragging cable, and dropped to the ground. Rolling out of the main aisle, he held his breath as Bokat dashed into the dim arcade.

"You can't get away." Bokat reached for the lamp control, then changed his mind. Lights would attract attention to his deadly game of hide-and-seek. Taking a security chip from his pocket, the Ferengi started toward the door.

Coiling the cable around the headpiece, Jake put the device on his head and flipped the visor screen up so he could see. He needed both hands free, and he wasn't going to leave the evidence of Bokat's treachery behind. Besides, his friends' lives depended on getting the game to Dr. Bashir. Jake couldn't overpower Bokat, but he was faster. Once he was on the Promenade, he could call for help. But first he had to stop Bokat from locking the door.

Frantic, Jake scanned the consoles within easy reach. Laser War, a late twentieth-century sharpshooter game, stood right behind him. Rising slightly, Jake lifted the laser pistol from a slot on the side. Credit codes were

only necessary to activate the scoreboard. The guns and targets were always on.

Tracking Bokat's progress down a side aisle, Jake sighted on another laser-activated game along the Ferengi's route. He fired just as Bokat came abreast of it, hitting the bull's-eye. A siren wailed, bells rang, and lights flashed. Bokat jumped with a startled cry and hit the deck. Jake scrambled to the far right wall, improving his position for a dash to freedom.

Bokat recovered quickly. Jumping to his feet, he scanned the room as he continued toward the door.

Jake was running out of time, but not out of options. He was squatting by Target-Ball, a primitive game that involved rolling hard balls up an alley and into circular cups. The smaller the cup, the higher the score. Jake keyed in his credit code and braced himself as eleven balls rolled into a long tray.

The clattering noise alerted Bokat, and he quickened his pace. Grabbing two balls, Jake aimed and hurled them. The first hit Bokat in the shoulder and stopped him cold. *High and inside,* Jake thought. The second just missed, but Bokat whirled toward the attack. *Strike.* A third ball smacked into the Ferengi's chest. Bokat exhaled loudly and staggered. *Walk.* If he got out of the arcade alive, he'd have to work on his pitching skills next time he and his father played baseball in Quark's holosuites. The fourth grazed a large Ferengi ear and smashed into the pinball machine behind him. *Foul.* Sparks flew, and so did Jake.

Armed with the remaining seven balls, Jake ran, throwing quickly and wildly. Half the balls missed, but the barrage kept Bokat unbalanced as Jake raced the remaining few feet to the door.

Stumbling and sliding over the balls strewn on the floor, Bokat screamed, "Stop—thief! Thief!"

Jake burst through the door and collided with Odo.

"In a hurry, Mr. Sisko?"

CHAPTER 6

Don't let him get away!" Bokat shrieked. "He broke into my arcade and stole a valuable piece of equipment!"

"Really?" Odo eyed the device perched on Jake's head. An elastic arm snaked out, and Odo's hand clamped on Jake's shoulder. "Not so fast, young man."

Out of breath from his narrow escape, Jake couldn't speak or resist when Odo took the game off his head. He concentrated on calming his pounding heart and racing pulse as Odo pulled him back toward the arcade.

"Excellent work, Mr. Odo!" Bokat plastered an ingratiating smile on his face. "Now that you've caught the burglar, I would like my property back—if you don't mind."

"I do mind. It's evidence." A large pocket formed in Odo's uniform, and he tucked the headpiece inside. With a casual glance at the door, Odo stepped inside. He picked up one of the balls scattered on the floor. "No signs of forced entry, but it looks as if there was a struggle."

Nervous now, Bokat became defensive. "Of course there was a struggle! I caught the boy stealing. Arrest him! I want my property back!"

Jake shook his head emphatically and managed a strangled, "Not stealing, Odo. Danger . . . in the back—"

"And vandalism!" Bokat cut Jake off and pointed to the broken pinball machine. "Just look at this mess! Shouldn't we be going to the security office? I want to file charges. And I want my game back."

Jake knew Bokat didn't want Odo to enter the back room. The Ferengi was stalling for time so he could destroy the data chips. The recordings would implicate him in the children's accidents and comas. There wasn't any other solid evidence.

"It's not a game, Odo!" Jake said in desperation. "It's an alien treasure map, and Nog—" Too late, Jake realized that mentioning Nog was the *wrong* thing to do. The Ferengi boy was an incorrigible troublemaker and a constant source of irritation for station security, especially Odo.

"Nog? That figures." Odo turned abruptly and whisked Jake onto the Promenade. "You, too, Bokat."

"By all means. That's a priceless antique, incredibly valuable." Like Jake, Bokat had to jog to keep pace with Odo's long stride. "I want it returned immediately, without delay. . . ."

"Shut up," Odo snapped, then added a sarcastic "please." Tugging on Jake's arm to hurry him along, the security officer touched his comm badge. "Odo to Sisko. We have a problem."

Arguing with Odo was useless, and Jake didn't try. His father would listen. He just hoped it wouldn't be too late.

Benjamin Sisko studied the alien headpiece with a skeptical frown.

Jake sat quietly, knowing his frantic explanation had sounded preposterous. Somehow, he had to convince Sisko and Odo to retrieve the tapes from Bokat's back room before the Ferengi erased them. Jake couldn't back up his fantastic story without that evidence, and crucial minutes had already been lost.

"Jake doesn't lie," Sisko said evenly.

"Oh, come now, Commander." Bokat rolled his eyes. "He doesn't want to be punished for grand larceny *and* disobeying you! You banned him from the games. He broke into the arcade to play. The shop was closed. No one was around. Who would know, right? He took the headpiece and panicked when I caught him."

"I did not break in!" Jake said hotly. "I fell in—by accident. The door wasn't locked."

Odo stared at the scowling merchant. "Rather careless of you, Bokat, leaving your door unlocked."

Bokat shrugged and shifted in his seat. "Perhaps, but it doesn't excuse the boy's crime. He stole a rare antique."

Sisko's dark eyes narrowed. He moved nearer, towering over Bokat. "Closing down during the height of the business day strikes me as rather odd, too—for a Ferengi."

Bokat fidgeted uncomfortably. "I had other, more profitable affairs to attend to."

"Yeah," Jake said. "Like dumping Nog's body somewhere."

"I protest!" Bokat's face reddened. "That's an absurd lie!"

"Duly noted," Sisko said calmly, then turned to Jake. "Tell me everything that happened again, from the beginning."

Jake took a deep breath and spoke slowly. "I was worried about Nog. Bokat had offered to let us play a game called the Zhodran Crystal Quest—for free."

A dent appeared over Odo's right eye as he started in surprise. "Did you say 'free'?"

"I can explain that—" Bokat sat forward suddenly, then fell back when Sisko roared.

"Later, Bokat!"

Jake continued at his father's nod. "I was suspicious, too. So I went to check. That's all, Dad. You said I couldn't play. You didn't say I couldn't *go* to the Games Bazaar."

"A fine distinction, but true," Sisko conceded. "Go on."

Jake related his story without further interruption. When he was finished, Sisko and Odo paused to reconsider the situation.

"So, you think this—game is responsible for the Selay boy's and Tena Lin's accidents?" Odo asked.

"Yes. The comas, too." Jake's gaze flicked hopefully between the two adults.

"Did Bokat offer to let them play it?" Sisko asked.

"I don't know. Bokat told me and Nog not to tell anyone." Jake sighed, desperate now. "Where is Nog anyway? We've got to find him! He was bitten by a snake, and he's probably comatose, too!" Jake looked at his father. "Please, believe me!"

Sisko met Jake's pleading gaze and tapped his comm badge. "Computer. Locate the Ferengi boy, Nog."

The computer reported in crisp, clipped tones. *"The Ferengi Nog is leaving Quark's Place."*

Sisko looked at Jake with sincere regret. "Apparently, Nog is alive and well on the Promenade."

Jake frowned, puzzled. Why was Nog okay while Lin and Rotor were lying in the Infirmary unconscious?

Bokat jumped up. "Can I go now?"

Odo nodded, then slapped his hand over Bokat's as the Ferengi reached for the device. "I have no reason to hold you, but I think I'll keep this for the time being."

"No!" Jake sprang to his feet. "If you let him go, he'll erase the data chips!"

The shapeshifter looked up suddenly, his neck stretching slightly as he peered past Sisko toward the office windows. Jake turned and gasped. Rom was running toward the Infirmary, carrying Nog's limp body. His best friend *was* trapped in the alien game!

"Correction, Bokat," Odo said. "You're not going anywhere just yet. You have some explaining to do."

"I have nothing to say." Bokat set his jaw stubbornly.

"Obstructing an investigation, Bokat?" Sisko grinned. "Odo has remarkable success getting answers to difficult questions from reluctant suspects. I've never asked how

he does it. He gets results. Come on, Jake." Sisko headed toward the door, carrying the headpiece.

Jake glanced back as Odo shifted into the familiar shape of a white-robed mythical Ferengest. The Ferengi believed the hooded ancestral spirit with glowing red eyes brought bad luck and poverty to descendants who violated Ferengi ethics. An alien that looked like a Ferengest had once befriended Jake, but Nog still had nightmares about Dhraako.

Bokat fell on his knees and grabbed Sisko's leg. "Don't leave me here with him! Please, I beg you. Have mercy!"

Sisko shook loose of the Ferengi's hold and kept walking. "I suggest you start talking, Bokat."

Dr. Bashir and Miles O'Brien entered Bokat's back room just as Sisko and the science officer, Jadzia Dax, finished reviewing Nog's encounter with the snake. All agreed that the correlations between the recordings and the accidents were too exact to be coincidences. Tena Lin had been burned severely. In the game she was surrounded by fire. Rotor had fallen into a ravine. He had a broken leg. The mysterious alien device was—somehow—responsible.

Feeling miserable, Jake sat on the floor by the wall. He was glad his father and the other senior officers believed him, but that wasn't enough to help his friends. Maybe nothing would.

"Jake was correct, Commander," Dr. Bashir said. "Nog's blood was infected with a biological poison. I neutralized it, but he's still in a coma—just like Rotor and Tena Lin."

"At least we know it's not an undetectable virus," O'Brien said. "One more minute in confinement with that Selay, and Odo would be arresting me for assault."

"Where is Captain Gaynor now, Doctor?" Sisko asked.

"I sent him back to his ship—until we know what's going on. The Selay can be a bit . . . destructive when they're angry."

"What did happen to those kids, Commander?" O'Brien asked.

Sisko explained Jake's theory while Dr. Bashir and O'Brien watched the replay of the accidents.

"How they were hurt doesn't matter now, Dad." Jake stood up and stared at the troubled adult faces surrounding him. "Dr. Bashir cured their physical injuries. We have to figure out how to get their conscious minds out of the game matrix."

"Can I see that thing, Commander?" O'Brien took the headpiece from Sisko. "Are you saying their minds are caught in this contraption, Jake?"

"Yes. Bokat said they were lost forever."

O'Brien scowled as he studied the artifact. He was a technological expert, one of the finest engineers in Starfleet, and he looked completely baffled. Jake's hopes slipped lower.

"Bokat may be right." Dax stared at the monitors, her pretty mouth set in a hard, grim line. "I've heard about the Zhodran and the Da-hahn Crystal legend."

"Anything that might help?" Sisko asked.

Jake listened attentively. Even though the trill host, Jadzia, was young, the symbiont inside her, Dax, was three hundred years old. Jadzia had three centuries of knowledge and memory at her disposal. She might know something important.

"The Zhodran are a very reclusive species," Dak explained. "They avoid any contact with outsiders. They believe the Da-hahn Crystal endows whoever possesses it with great power and eternal life. But—it's just a legend. There's no proof the crystal actually exists."

"But the game exists," Sisko observed.

"A map, actually," Jake interjected. "The location of the crystal is disclosed at the end of the quest."

"Where did Bokat get such a dangerous device?" Dr. Bashir stepped aside as Odo walked through the door.

"Probably stole it from the Zhodran," O'Brien quipped.

"Someone did," Dax said.

"But not Bokat," Odo said confidently. "He bought it from an Orion pirate three years ago for six bars of gold-pressed latinum. The Orion couldn't figure out how to activate the device. Bokat was successful. I would know if he were lying."

"I agree with Odo, Benjamin," Dax said. "The artifact's been missing for three decades. The library contained only one reference to the Da-hahn Crystal or an associated device. Thirty years ago, the Crown of Ultimate Wisdom was stolen from Zhodran's archives by persons unknown. It's never been recovered."

Sisko frowned. "It has now."

"And it's our only hope of bringing those children out of their comas." Dr. Bashir looked pointedly at O'Brien. "That's your department, Chief."

"I'll be honest, I don't have a clue how this thing works." O'Brien turned the device so Julian could see the interior surface. "I'm assuming these filament contacts pierce the scalp and draw on the brain's energies. Taking the game apart might shatter the mechanism holding the impulses."

"If their neural patterns are trapped," Sisko said. "Their brains might have been . . . short-circuited, in a manner of speaking, and the impulses destroyed by the device."

Appalled, Dr. Bashir pressed Sisko. "I must insist that we proceed as though the minds are imprisoned and still viable."

Sisko relented. "Agreed. Any ideas how?"

"It's not like a transporter," O'Brien said. "There's no control panel."

No one had any suggestions, and the silence of bewildered indecision forced Jake to act. Forgotten in the shadows during the discussion, he stepped forward and spoke boldly.

"Someone has to go in and get them."

CHAPTER 7

Jake skipped to keep up with the parade of senior officers crossing the bustling Promenade. At Jake's request, O'Brien had contacted Keiko to meet them. Odo had returned to duty, and the remaining adults were so involved in a dialogue about the Zhodran device and the bizarre consequences of wearing it, no one had asked *why* he wanted to go to the school. But they would. As soon as someone thought to ask the right question.

"Sending someone into this game is not like sending an away team down to a planet." Sisko stared at the floor as he walked. "We're not dealing with physical circumstances, but with *thought.*"

"But it *is* the same," Jake insisted. "In a way."

"I think Jake is right," Dax said, matching Sisko's stride. "When we encounter a problem in the physical world, we decide how to solve it with our *minds.*"

"Quite true." Dr. Bashir smiled agreeably at Dax. "If someone is lying at the bottom of a pit with a broken leg, we'd *think* about how to get the victim out first, before we actually did it. The only difference with the game is that the *doing* takes place in the mind, too."

Sisko was still not convinced. "But this *game* is dangerous. It traps the electrical impulses that generate conscious thought, if someone makes the wrong decisions."

Dax smiled and shook her head slightly. "Benjamin, the point of the game is to make the *right* decisions."

"Exactly!" Jake exclaimed.

Dax winked at Jake. "And luck is not a factor. There's no toss of the dice, no random selection of cards or spin of a wheel. Success depends strictly on intelligence and skill in problem solving. The player relies on his ability —not chance."

"I'll buy that," O'Brien said, "but I don't understand how you expect another player to free the trapped children."

Everyone came to a stop outside the school. Keiko wasn't there yet.

Jake quickly explained his idea. "If the new player avoids the traps that caught Rotor and Lin and Nog, he can probably find a way to rescue them from the bridge and the pit and the snake."

Sisko frowned uncertainly, and O'Brien nodded thoughtfully.

"It's just a theory," Jake said desperately, "but escape solutions are programmed into every game I've ever played. Otherwise, they wouldn't be worth playing."

"Escape is not just a matter of solving the riddles and problems, Jake," O'Brien said. "The trapped impulses need a way to get *out* of the device." Light sparkled across the silver surface of the headpiece as O'Brien held it up for dramatic effect. "Four minds. One device."

"Only one road home." Dr. Bashir sighed.

"Could you replicate the device?" Sisko asked.

"In a Cardassian replicator?" O'Brien snorted and rolled his eyes. "I wouldn't advise it. Besides, replication might destroy the conscious impulses. We can't risk it."

"I've thought about that, too." Jake paused as Keiko rounded the corner with her sleepy daughter Molly cradled in her arms.

"Sorry I took so long. I had to get Molly dressed. What's going on?" Keiko unlocked the classroom, and everyone filed inside. Jake immediately ran to a corner storage cabinet and pulled out the Federation IQ/ Aptitude helmet. He rushed back to join the group, then had to wait to get their attention.

"A separate conduit is needed for each neural pattern," Dr. Bashir finished explaining to Keiko. "We've only got one."

"Two!" Jake shoved the helmet into O'Brien's free hand. "And this one *can* be replicated."

"What is it?" Dr. Bashir asked.

"A Federation testing device," O'Brien muttered. He glanced at Dax. "What do you think? Will it work?"

Dax examined both headpieces, then nodded. "I think so. Bokat adapted the cable connections to be compatible with a standard recorder. I'm sure we can integrate three Federation helmets with the alien design to open extra impulse channels."

Excited by the technological challenge of beating the alien gadget at its own game, O'Brien grinned. "The

Zhodran device will function as a control panel. The thoughts of the person wearing it will direct everything that happens."

"Who's going to wear it?" Dr. Bashir asked.

"I'm the best man for the job." All heads snapped around to stare at Jake. "I passed the IQ/Aptitude test with above-average marks, and nobody has topped my scores in the arcade."

"Absolutely not!" Sisko gripped Jake's shoulders. "This is not just another game. This device hurts people. It doesn't keep a running score. It's win or lose. Nothing in between."

"I know that, Dad, but the rules are the same. It's possible to win, and I can do it!"

Sisko was adamant. "Three children have already been hurt. We're not going to make it four!"

"But, I'm the best—"

"No!"

"If I may, Commander," O'Brien interjected cautiously. Sisko's eyes flashed, but he let O'Brien speak. "We can't discount Jake's ability. I've tried those games —without much success, I'm afraid. I don't have the reflexes, the quick response factor that comes naturally to someone Jake's age."

"Chief O'Brien." Drawing himself up to his full height, Sisko glared at his Chief of Operations. "If we were talking about Molly, would you let her risk her life?"

"Molly's only three years old!" Jake protested. "I'm fourteen—old enough to make this decision."

"Jake's growing up, Commander," Keiko said gently. "Sooner or later you'll have to let go."

Sisko smiled sadly. "I'd prefer later."

O'Brien touched Molly's cheek. "I'm sure we will, too, when the time comes."

"My friends are in trouble, Dad," Jake said earnestly. "I'm the best chance they've got, and I want to help."

Throwing up his hands, Sisko barked, "All right! But I insist we take every possible precaution."

"No problem." Playfully cuffing Jake, O'Brien started for the door. "I've got a couple of safeguards in mind."

Solemnly Jake offered his hand to his father. "Thanks, Dad. I won't let you down."

"See that you don't," Sisko snapped sternly. His expression softened as he shook Jake's hand.

Jake flushed with pride. Having his father's respect and confidence felt great. The only thing that could feel better was getting his friends out of the Zhodran Crystal Quest alive.

CHAPTER 8

Sitting on a biobed, Jake watched Dax, O'Brien, and Dr. Bashir complete their preparations. Once he put on the headpiece, his own life would be in danger, too. He *was* scared—but fear gave him an edge. He would be alert and ready to cope with any problem the alien game presented.

Jake's chest tightened as he looked at Nog. No trace of animated excitement showed on the Ferengi boy's pale face. No mischievous plans were hatching behind the blank eyes. He just lay there, unmoving and quiet, wearing a Federation helmet modified to fit over his large skull and ears. The extended neural network would not be activated until the filaments in the Zhodran artifact made contact with Jake's brain.

Then Nog's fate, like Tena Lin's and Rotor's, would be in Jake's hands. *Or thoughts,* Jake corrected himself. Now he understood the crushing pressure Benjamin Sisko lived with every day. Everyone on the station depended on his father's decisions.

Nog's father had stopped by to demand that Dr. Bashir get Nog back on his feet as soon as possible. Quark was making Rom do double duty as waiter and busboy. However, Jake knew that was just an excuse to get away from the busy bar. Rom was really worried about his comatose son.

Captain Gaynor and Tena Lin's parents had come into the Infirmary a short time later, pressing for information and action. Dr. Bashir had handled them diplomatically, expressing high hopes for the children's complete recovery. Then he had explained that having upset parents lurking about would hamper the treatment process. At first they had refused to leave, but Dr. Bashir had finally convinced them. Jake was uncomfortable being the center of scientific and medical attention. Being watched by emotionally involved parents would have made the stress unbearable.

"Almost ready, Jake." O'Brien connected the Zhodran device to the data-chip recorder. Bokat's equipment had been confiscated to save time. Commander Sisko had insisted on monitoring Jake's progress through the game. If something went wrong, the officers could analyze Jake's actions to avoid making the same mistakes. Benjamin Sisko would attempt the rescue in the event Jake failed.

But he was not going to fail. He was the best player on Deep Space Nine. He would beat the Zhodran Crystal Quest and save his friends. He absolutely had to—for reasons that went far beyond the satisfaction of winning. It was a matter of life and death.

"How are you feeling?" Sisko walked up to Jake, trying very hard not to look as worried as he felt.

"Fine." Jake sighed. "A little nervous, maybe."

"Nothing unusual about that." Leaning forward slightly, Sisko whispered, "I always get nervous when it's time for Starfleet's senior officer evaluations. Butterflies, cold sweats, bad dreams, sick to my stomach. It's awful."

"Really?" Jake sat back, surprised. His father was the hard, demanding commander of Deep Space Nine. Oddly, knowing that the self-assured elder Sisko had moments of anxiety bolstered Jake's spirits and confidence. "Being evaluated makes you sick?"

"Worse than diplomatic receptions." Smiling tightly, Sisko stepped aside as O'Brien and Dr. Bashir came forward with the alien headpiece. Dax remained by the console that integrated the Federation helmets with the Zhodran device.

"All right, Jake," Dr. Bashir said pleasantly. "There's nothing to worry about. The biobed will monitor all your physical responses. The second an injury registers, I'll be right here to take care of it." The young man flinched as O'Brien shot him a warning look and kicked him in the lower leg. "Not that I expect anything to happen, of course," Dr. Bashir sputtered. "It's just a precaution, you understand."

"Of course." Jake was very much aware that a lot could go wrong, but knowing Dr. Bashir was there to fix any injuries eased some of the tension. "I'll be fine. It might even be fun."

"Sure it will. Look at it as a great adventure." O'Brien

held up the Crown of Ultimate Wisdom. "I'm ready when you are."

Jake nodded and stretched out on the biobed. *Ready or not, here I come,* he thought as O'Brien placed the silver device on his head. A warm tingling spread over his scalp just before everything went dark.

Commander Benjamin Sisko had never felt so helpless. His only child was embarking on a dangerous mission—alone. Making difficult decisions was part of growing up, and Sisko could not deny Jake's right to take responsibility. Jake was exceptionally talented and skilled at this type of game. Still, if anything happened to him, Sisko would never forgive himself.

"He's in, Commander," Dax reported from the integration console. "Federation connections are activated."

Sisko's heart lurched as Jake's facial features went slack.

"Vital signs normal and holding steady." Dr. Bashir stood on the other side of the biobed, surrounded by emergency medical equipment. "Alpha brain-wave activity is not registering."

Sisko nodded in acknowledgment. This was not an unexpected development. Jake's conscious mind had been transferred into the alien circuitry of the Zhodran device. The boy was on his own.

"Commander!" O'Brien called out. "I'm getting a visual."

Turning abruptly, Sisko stared at the portable monitor and a picture of a forest as seen through Jake's eyes. A bed of pine needles cushioned a trail winding through a woodland of majestic trees. Sparkling dust motes danced in rays of sunlight that streamed through green-leafed branches. A red bird soared from a high perch with a shrill cry, scolding Jake for disturbing the wilderness peace. A small, furry animal with alert brown eyes and a twitching nose darted across the path. A brook ran parallel to the trail, splashing over rocks flecked with glittering crystals.

"I'm sorry," Dr. Bashir said sharply. "The Infirmary is temporarily closed except for extreme emergencies."

Sisko glanced over his shoulder with a frown. A humanoid alien he did not recognize paused in the doorway. The tall, slim man wore high black boots over royal-blue tights and a short, white-furred cape over a matching tunic. Startling blue eyes dominated a beautiful face framed in long silken white hair. He carried a silver rod with flickering blue lights in one hand and a wide leather thong in the other. Ignoring Dr. Bashir, the alien advanced. A faint humming sound sang from the silver rod.

Furious, Sisko moved to stop the alien. No distractions could be tolerated. "This area is currently off-limits—"

Spotting the monitor, the alien screeched and twirled the folded leather thong above his head. A pocket in the middle of the strap whipped through the air. With a snap he released one end, sending a white rock skimming across the room. Sisko ducked, but the monitor screen shattered in a blast of sparks and glass.

Dr. Bashir hit his comm badge. "Odo! To the Infirmary. Now! Hostile alien intruder!"

"What the—!" Sisko stumbled backward as the alien dropped the slingshot, pushed past him, and lunged toward Jake. Fearing for Jake's safety, Sisko sprang and grabbed the man around the waist. They fell on the floor in a tangle of thrashing arms and legs. The alien shrieked, twisting and kicking under Sisko's bulk. Heavier than the slim humanoid, Sisko kept him pinned down until Odo appeared and snatched the silver rod. The alien stopped struggling instantly.

Major Kira ran in a moment later. She paused, looked at Sisko, then Odo, and shrugged. "Well, it looks as if you two have things under control here."

"More or less," Sisko said breathlessly.

"His ship isn't armed, Commander. Neither was he, according to my sensors," Kira said defensively. "I had no idea he was a threat until I heard Dr. Bashir's call for Security."

Odo picked up the fallen slingshot and handed it to Kira. "Primitive, but effective, Major."

Nodding, Kira inspected the leather strap. "And made of harmless natural materials. The weapon detectors aren't calibrated to suspect a device like this."

Rising to his feet, Sisko quickly looked at the team following Jake's progress. "Status report."

"The Zhodran device and the Federation helmets are operating perfectly," Dax said calmly.

"Jake's physical readings are still normal, too." Dr. Bashir spoke without taking his gaze away from the biobed sensors.

"But we've lost visual contact." O'Brien's fist

slammed into the broken monitor cabinet. "There's nothing I can do to fix this, Commander."

So far, Jake was all right. But for how long? Checking his temper, Sisko hauled the alien to his feet and glared into blazing blue eyes. "I am Commander Benjamin Sisko, the Starfleet administrator of this space station. Who are you?"

The alien tensed, then relaxed with a serene sigh. "I am Talarn, High Priest of the Zhodran Temple of Light."

"Why did you attack my son?"

The priest glanced at Jake. "That one wears the Crown of Ultimate Wisdom. I've been searching for it since it was stolen from the Temple of Light many years ago."

"How did you know it was here?" Major Kira asked curiously.

"May I?" Talarn addressed Odo, extending an open hand toward the silver rod.

Sisko nodded, and the security officer reluctantly gave the dazzling artifact back to the Zhodran. The humming grew louder when the priest pointed it at Jake. The blue lights brightened and flashed faster.

"All these years," Talarn said, "the locator staff has been dark and silent. I have been wandering from star to star looking for the crown. When it was finally activated, the rod responded, and I tracked it here. The Crown of Ultimate Wisdom is the sacred property of Zhodran. You must return it immediately."

"I recognize your claim, Talarn." Calmer now, Sisko adopted a diplomatic tone. "And the crown will be returned—after my son and three other children are separated from the neural matrix."

Talarn shook his head sadly. "They cannot return, Benjamin Sisko. To escape the power of the crown, the mind must overcome many obstacles and make the right decision at the journey's end."

"We're aware of that." Sisko motioned toward Dax and the integration console. "Additional conduits have been attached to the crown to provide safe passage for all the children's minds."

"Ingenious, but futile." Talarn paused, then added in a somber whisper. "It has never been done."

"Never's a long time," Kira scoffed.

The high priest remained unruffled. "The Zhodran are a quiet people, and mistrustful of outsiders. However, our planet is located in a crowded, highly traveled sector of space."

Sisko listened patiently. Dax had explained that the Zhodran were isolationists who feared everything foreign.

"For two thousand years representatives of many alien species have tried to solve the puzzle of the crown. Passing this test is required to open diplomatic and trade relations with Zhodran."

Sisko frowned darkly as the meaning of the priest's words became clear. "Are you saying no one has successfully completed this test in two thousand years?"

"Yes." Talarn scanned the gathering with genuine regret. "The journey is riddled with tasks designed to test the character of the individual chosen to represent their species. Qualities such as honesty, courage, compassion—all are measured. Many get far, but no one ever makes the right judgment in the end. Only the high priest and his designated successor know the correct response, a secret that has been guarded for generations."

Stunned, Sisko just stared at him.

"The mind becomes trapped, and eventually it simply fades out of existence." A tear ran down the Zhodran's cheek as he gazed on the bodies of the children. "They are lost."

"No." Sisko turned to look at Jake's still face. "This game is not over yet."

CHAPTER 9

Even though Jake knew he was hooked up to a virtual reality device, it seemed as if he had really been transported to the Zhodran world. *A beautiful world,* Jake thought when he awakened in the middle of a lush forest. The tall trees and clear, running stream reminded him of Earth. He had gone trout fishing once in an Adirondack river—on the holodeck of the *Saratoga*. But holosimulations were only images of reality, and this world wasn't real, either. It was just an illusion taking place in his mind.

Still, it felt real, and Jake eagerly started down the winding path. The scenery was a refreshing change from the somber gray halls of the Cardassian-built space station, and the challenge written into the rules teased his competitive spirit. The Zhodran Crystal Quest promised to be a thrilling adventure most players could only dream about. Then he remembered that his best friend and two other children were trapped within the

63

matrix. The results of playing were real, too—and dangerous.

Knowing that Dax, O'Brien, Dr. Bashir, and his father were watching was a comfort. If he did make a mistake, they would not abandon him in the alien game.

Don't think about failure, Jake admonished himself. A winner was positive and confident, and he was going to win.

The trees began to thin out, and soon the trail left the woods to meander up a grassy slope. At the top of the knoll, Jake paused and gasped. He dropped to the ground, his heart hammering wildly against his ribs. A calm lake stretched before him. Tena Lin was trapped on a burning bridge to the left. Straight ahead, a rowboat was tethered to a wooden dock guarded by—a Borg.

"Oh, no . . ." Jake slid backward on his stomach, shaking his head and trembling with fear. Not a Borg. Anything but a Borg. It had been three years since the biological-mechanical aliens had attacked the Federation Fleet at Wolf 359. His father, first officer under the Vulcan Captain Storil, had been on the bridge when the huge, cube-shaped Borg ship fired on the *U.S.S. Saratoga.* Jake and his mother had been in their quarters when an explosion ripped the deck apart and sent a broken bulkhead down upon them. Fire. Jake remembered flames leaping upward from the level below and the crashing sound of heavy metal. Then he had blacked out. His next memory was waking up in a hospital bed with his father sitting by his side. His mother had died on the ship.

The nightmares didn't happen so often now, but they

were always there—dreadful images of giant box ships and mechanical men—waiting in the depths of his mind to attack him in sleep.

This time he was wide awake. He could not hide or run. He had to face the Borg, or Tena Lin would never escape the fire or the game matrix. Taking a deep breath, Jake surveyed the layout of the land. Maybe he could avoid the deadly Borg sentry.

Jake studied the burning bridge. The Bajoran girl was hard to see through the fire and smoke, but she had made it halfway across before the flames had cut her off. Unable to advance or retreat, she was stuck in the middle of the blazing inferno. Jake could not use the bridge, either. He would be caught in the fire, too, and they'd both be trapped.

But he could swim. It wasn't that far, and once he reached the bridge, he could coax Tena Lin into jumping off. She'd have to leap through the burning wall, but even if her clothes caught fire, falling into the water would extinguish the flames. First, he had to get to the lake, and there were no bushes or trees to provide cover. The Borg might spot him, but that was a chance he had to take. Individual Borg were very single-minded and ignored everything but the immediate task. If Jake didn't go near the dock, maybe this one would ignore him.

Crawling on arms and knees, Jake moved down the slope on his stomach. The Borg guardian of the dock did not seem to notice him. It stared straight ahead, the energy weapon built onto its right arm raised and ready. *So far so good. . . .*

Solid ground suddenly squished, and Jake's elbow

sank into dark brown ooze. "Yuck." Jake wrinkled his nose. The stench of rotting grass and other organics fouled the mud. A sucking *slurp* cut the quiet as he pulled his arm out of the muck. Jake wondered if the whole lake was surrounded by the bog. A moment later he realized the size of the awful-smelling mire was irrelevant.

Something sharp stung his thigh. He swallowed a yelp of pain, scooted back onto dry ground, and rolled onto his side. A small, amphibious creature that resembled a blue frog with a spotted dorsal fin was attached to his leg by its teeth. It suddenly began to chomp with ravenous hunger.

The carnivorous little beast was trying to eat him! Jake grabbed the frog, yanked it off, and hurled it into the still water. Scrambling backward, Jake watched in horror as the water came alive. Thousands of Zhodran frogs rocketed into the air. They came in various shades of blue and green, and ranged in size from a couple of inches to over a foot long. The lake teemed with the creatures, and they all had snapping, pointed teeth that could strip the flesh from a boy's bones in less than five minutes.

Jake was not going swimming.

Dropping his head onto crossed arms, Jake moaned. Unless he wanted to forsake his friends and force his father to risk his life in the game, he had to face the Borg. There was no other way to get to the rowboat. At least the Borg would just blast him to smithereens. It didn't want him as the main course for dinner.

Resigned, Jake paused to consider the situation. A Borg stood between him and the rowboat, which he needed to rescue Lin and get to the far shore. The tools to accomplish the task had to be programmed into the game. Defeating the Borg might be difficult, but not impossible. He just had to figure out how.

A large purple bruise appeared around the bite wound, then began to disappear. Apparently, back in the Infirmary, Dr. Bashir was on the job. The sting faded to an irritating itch, and Jake turned his attention to the Borg. Rising to his feet, he strode boldly across the grass toward the dock.

The sentry did not react until Jake hit a strip of sand separating the grass from the water. "Halt and be assimilated," the Borg said in a flat monotone. "Resistance is futile."

My eye, Jake thought. The *Enterprise* had arrived at Wolf 359 too late to save most of the Fleet, but the crew had destroyed the Borg ship and saved Earth. As long as he was still alive and thinking, nothing was futile. He quickly stepped back onto the grass and stumbled over a rusty, metal chest he hadn't noticed before. The Borg resumed its silent, watchful stance. Jake touched the sand with his toe.

"Halt and be—"

The Borg stopped talking the moment Jake retreated from the beach. He suspected the game had materialized the chest once his intention to approach the dock had been established. Now that he knew the Borg would ignore him, he could examine the contents of the chest without worrying about being shot . . . or assimilated.

Stressed metal creaked as Jake opened the box. There were two items inside: a Klingon disrupter and a

Federation-issue electronic tuner. O'Brien used a similar device to calibrate sensors on Deep Space Nine. Again, Jake stopped to think.

Challenge the Borg or forfeit. Defeat the Borg or lose. Every game he had ever played provided the tools necessary to win. They also incorporated tricks designed to trap an anxious, unwary player. Only one of the items was the right one. Which one?

The Klingon disrupter would short-circuit the Borg's systems, killing it, but the weapon lacked the precision of a Federation phaser. The beam might also destroy the dock and the rowboat. Besides, the idea of killing anything turned Jake's stomach sour.

He picked up the tuner and studied the frequency control. The instrument could be set to transmit at different wavelengths. Of course! All Borg were in constant communication with every other Borg. Isolated from the collective mind, an individual could not function. Jake did not have to kill the Borg to succeed. Gripping the tuner, he stepped onto the beach.

"Halt and be assimilated. Resistance is futile."

The Borg lowered its weapon and took aim. Armed only with a maintenance tool, Jake frantically shifted frequencies. If he didn't hit the right one soon, the game would be over, and he would be trapped. No fate could be worse than spending eternity as a member of the Borg collective.

"Halt and be assimilated. Resistance is fu—"

Jake jerked his hand off the touch-pad. The Borg was frozen, its expression blank.

It worked!

Shaking, Jake kept the transmitter pointed at the sentry as he slipped past. He untied the rowboat and stepped in. Hundreds of hungry frogs skimmed through the water just beneath the surface. Still aiming the tuner, Jake sat down on the center seat and gently pushed off with his free hand.

When the boat had drifted clear, Jake set the tuner on the aft seat and reached for the oars. His hand slipped on the smooth wood, and the broad end of the right oar smacked the water. A dozen frogs leaped from the lake. Two landed in the boat and hopped toward Jake for a quick nibble. He dispatched them quickly, throwing them far from the boat. All that holosuite pitching practice had sure been coming in handy lately.

Sounds that were muted on land carried loudly over the water. Tena Lin's screams rose above the roaring fire, assaulting Jake's ears. Forced to row with careful, deliberate strokes, the slow journey to the bridge tried his patience. Dip. Pull. Up. Back. He didn't dare go faster. The slightest ripple would send the blue frogs leaping in a frenzy. And surely Dr. Bashir was healing Lin's burns as quickly as they appeared back in the Infirmary. Dip. Pull. He had to stay in one piece if he was going to help her. Up. Back. He steered toward a portion of the structure that wasn't in flames.

Finally the boat glided between two sturdy pillars supporting the bridge. Jake stared at the overhead planks and guided the boat toward the center of the span. Jumping into the water was no longer an option, either. The frogs would make short work of the tasty Bajoran girl. There had to be another way.

When he reached the burning span, Jake saw the trapdoor. It was open, and a ladder led down the side of a huge support pillar. Grabbing the ladder to anchor the boat, Jake hollered. "Tena Lin! It's Jake! Down here!"

Lin, her face covered with red blisters and black soot, peered through the square opening. "Jake! Thank the Prophets!" Without another word, she scrambled down the ladder.

"Carefully, Lin. It doesn't take much to set off these frog things." Nodding solemnly, Lin slowly stepped in and sat on the bow seat. The red blisters on her face and hands vanished, but the black soot remained. "Don't make any sudden moves, okay?"

"Okay." Lin exhaled softly. "Thanks for saving me, Jake. Rotor and Nog didn't even try. They just rowed to the other side of the lake."

Jake felt obliged to defend the two boys. "They thought this was just a game, Lin. They didn't know you were *really* trapped here. I did, and I could barely see you in the fire. I don't think they ignored you on purpose."

"Well, maybe not." She paused with a questioning frown. "You came here just to rescue me?"

Jake shrugged. "And Rotor and Nog. They're stuck in this game, too—somewhere."

"That was a brave thing to do." Lin smiled, then cocked her head. "How did you ever get past that terrible Cardassian?"

"What Cardassian?" Jake asked, puzzled.

"The one guarding the dock."

71

CHAPTER 10

Jake beached the boat on the far side of the lake. Anxious to leave the vicious blue frogs behind, he jumped for dry land, then took Lin's hand to help her out.

"So—you saw a Cardassian guarding the dock."

Lin shivered and scowled with disgust. "Yes. That's why I decided to take the bridge over the lake. Bad move, I guess."

Jake nodded, but said nothing. Tena Lin had seen a Cardassian—the feared and hated enemy of all Bajorans. And he had seen a Borg, a being Jake dreaded more than any other creature in the galaxy. Nog and Rotor had probably faced frightening beings, too, but they had overcome the dangers and moved further into the game. This put a whole new perspective on the rules. The game modified the program for each player.

Another trail angled across a rolling meadow toward a rocky ridge. Leading the way, Jake reflected on his new information. The game drew on a player's emotions and experiences to design specific traps for each individual.

Knowing this might make the difference between winning and losing.

The meadow path was smooth and flanked by clumps of bright flowers. A golden sun shown in a cloudless sky, bathing Jake in a relaxing warmth. By the time they reached the base of the sheer, vertical cliff, he felt refreshed.

"I can't climb that," Lin said.

"Why not?" Jake looked up. The top of the flat rock wall couldn't be seen from the ground.

Lin's jaw locked defiantly, then she sagged against the rock. "I'm afraid of heights." Her face paled and she began to shake.

Jake had not anticipated this problem. He wasn't thrilled about making the dangerous climb, either. He'd do it because he had to finish the mission and escape the game. But how could he force Tena Lin to attempt something that frightened her so badly?

"We have to move forward to win the game," Jake said.

"I don't care. I'll fall." Lin crossed her arms stubbornly.

Desperate, Jake's mind raced. He couldn't leave her behind, and he wasn't about to stay. He tried another tactic. The Bajoran girl did not know how the Zhodran device really worked. "This cliff is just another obstacle in a stupid game, Lin. Your body is in the Infirmary. If you fall, it's no big deal. Dr. Bashir is standing by to fix any injuries. But if you don't go on, your mind will be trapped here—forever."

Lin's eyes flashed. "I'm *not* climbing that cliff."

"Okay." Jake shrugged, smitten with a sudden brainstorm. He had to make Tena Lin mad enough to forget her fear. "Wait till I tell Rotor and Nog you gave up on a game without even trying! They'll never let you live it down!"

"You wouldn't dare!" Lin stood up, furious.

"Won't I?" Laughing, Jake scrambled to the first ledge. Above him, he spotted hand- and footholds. Below him, Lin exhaled in angry frustration and started up after him.

Jake scurried up the rock wall, staying just out of Lin's reach. The holds chiseled into the rock made the climb easy and safe. Even so, the Bajoran girl would probably stay angry for a while, but she was still with him. They both had a chance to get out of the treacherous game, and that was all that mattered.

That and being stranded in the middle of a cliff.

The handholds gave out fifty feet from the top. Jake waited for Lin on a wide ledge. Flat rock rose upward on either side of a jagged cleft cut into the mountain.

"You did that on purpose!" Lin scrambled onto the rocky shelf and collapsed to catch her breath.

"Guilty." Jake grinned sheepishly. "The good news is—we don't have to climb to the top."

Puzzled, Lin looked up at the smooth rockface and gasped. "Don't tell me have to climb back *down* this mountain!"

"No, we're going through it." Jake turned and ducked into the narrow passage. Lin stayed close on his heels as he felt his way through the dark corridor. When they emerged on another ledge, Jake stopped suddenly.

Lin bumped into his back. "Sorry."

"That's okay." Jake scanned the rugged, familiar

terrain. He knew from Bokat's recording that Rotor lay at the bottom of a deep canyon directly in front of them. The cliff wall that towered around them was just as steep and impassable as the one on the far side of the passage. However, two paths led off the ledge.

The left trail connected to a sturdy land bridge that spanned the chasm a short distance away. The right side of the shelf fell away in a sheer drop, and a rope bridge stretched from the ledge, across the ravine, to a flat mesa. The mesa stood alone in the center of the canyon, and the sides of both formations were as smooth as the cliff. The topography looked like a smaller version of the Grand Canyon back on Earth.

"How are we going to get down there?" Lin peered down at the unmoving Selay boy.

Jake shook his head, looked up, and stiffened.

"What?" Lin asked, alarmed.

Jake didn't answer. He was totally focused on Tommy Watson.

"Hey, Jake! Wanna fight?" The blond boy stood on the distant mesa. "Naw, guess not, huh? Daddy's little boy can't take a little pain. Right, Jakey-poo? Sissy Sisko!"

A year older, six inches taller, and forty pounds heavier than Jake, Tommy had made life miserable during his three years on Mars. Like Jake's father, Tommy's dad worked at the Utopia Planitia Yards rebuilding the fleet destroyed by the Borg. They lived in the same neighborhood, went to the same school, and hung out on the same playground. Tommy bullied everyone smaller than himself, but he had taken particular pleasure in picking on Jake.

And Jake had taken the abuse, day after day after day.

"Jake! What's wrong?" Lin asked nervously.

"Tommy Watson, that's what!" Jake clenched his teeth.

"Sissy Sisko, make a fist so—I can kick your butt!" Tommy laughed, then wagged his fingers. "Come and get me, Jake!"

"Who's Tommy Watson?" The small ridges on Lin's Bajoran nose pressed together in a bewildered frown.

"That kid over there!" Jake snapped and pointed to the isolated mesa. The rope bridge was the only access to the butte.

"What boy?"

Jake was seeing red and didn't hear Lin's baffled question. For three years Tommy had ridiculed, insulted, and threatened him. Smaller and younger, Jake had never fought back.

"Hey, Sisko! Whatsa matter? Chicken?"

But Jake had changed since moving to Deep Space Nine. He was older, stronger, and more confident. Tommy Watson couldn't insult him now and get away with it. Jake didn't care if Tommy landed a few painful punches. It was time to strike a blow for dignity.

"That's right, Jake," Tommy jeered. "Come and get me!"

Jake put one foot on the rope bridge and froze. Tommy Watson was back on Mars. The boy on the mesa was an illusion the game had fashioned from his memory to trick him into doing something dumb—and deadly. He stepped back and took a deep breath.

Back on Mars Jake had been afraid of Tommy. Hard to admit, but true. He wasn't afraid now. The insults were just words, spoken by a boy who used brute strength and intimidation to mask his insecurities. Jake didn't need to prove anything to anyone, especially himself. His dignity would survive Tommy Watson, and Rotor would survive the game, but only if Jake refused to fight.

Lin stared at him, confused. Jake realized she had not seen or heard Tommy. Unaware of his problem, the girl could not influence his actions. She and the others had had their chance and failed. Now they were just passengers on Jake's solitary quest.

"We have to go this way." Jake turned away from Tommy and headed down the left path.

On the far side of the land bridge Jake saw the steps. Invisible from the ledge, the carved-rock staircase curved down into the ravine. They reached Rotor in a couple of minutes.

The Selay boy was asleep. He awakened with a start when Jake shook him. "Jake! Lin! Am I glad to see you!" Rotor moved his leg carefully, as if he expected it to hurt.

"Dr. Bashir's already fused the bone, Rotor," Jake said.

"Is he here?" Rotor stood up, testing his healed injury.

Jake quickly explained the situation. "We have to find Nog and play to the end of this game before we can leave."

"You find Nog," Rotor said. "I'm getting out of here *now.*"

"I don't think so." The carved steps had recessed back into the canyon wall, and a rock slide blocked the canyon under the rope bridge, leaving only one path open. Jake turned and headed deeper into the winding canyon. Lin followed immediately. Rotor caught up a moment later.

"Who did you see on the mesa, Rotor?" Jake asked.

"An arrogant, stinking Antican. He dared me to fight him for the mountain. I could not refuse the challenge."

"Maybe you should have, Rotor. You ended up at the bottom of a canyon with a broken leg." Lin paused thoughtfully. "I was almost incinerated because I didn't face my fear of Cardassians."

Rotor shrugged. "The Anticans are the mortal enemy of Selay. Honor must be defended at all costs."

Honor was just another word for dignity and respect. Jake knew that sometimes people had to fight back, as when the Borg attacked the fleet on their way to capture Earth. But sometimes honor was better served by turning away. The Selay and the Anticans had been denied membership in the Federation because they could not settle their differences. There was no honor in that.

"Defending Selay honor almost cost your life, Rotor." Lin shook her head. "If you had just ignored him and walked away, you might have won the game. The Antican would have lost."

Rotor hesitated, troubled by Lin's observation. "This is true, Tena Lin. I will think about it."

Jake smiled as he led them through the twisting, rocky maze. Rotor had learned a valuable lesson. Maybe someday, the young Selay would help stop the war between his people and the Anticans.

Provided, of course, that Jake managed to free them from the Zhodran game.

CHAPTER II

The canyon walls gradually receded, and Jake led his companions onto a vast desert. The dry, sun-baked plain was not flat and lifeless like he expected. The rolling sands were littered with scrub brush and strange, grotesque trees with twisted branches and spines instead of leaves. Blue and gold lizards scampered into the brush as they passed. Large birds with leathery wings soared overhead, and a huge tortoise ambled on a slow but steady trek across a dune sprinkled with flaming orange flowers. Piles of massive, balanced rocks dotted the expanse.

"There's Nog!" Lin pointed excitedly.

Jake's gaze flicked toward a large mound surrounded by a sea of blue and gold flowers. Nog was flopped over a rock at the top.

Lin started to run.

"Wait!" Jake grabbed the girl's arm and dragged her to a stop. The game could fabricate dangers without warning, and they had come too far to take unnecessary chances. "We have to be careful, Lin."

Nodding, Lin fell back and let Jake move ahead. Nothing threatening popped out of the sand to stop them, but they were hot and sweaty when they finally reached the edge of the flower sea. However, a stretch of moving sand separated the thick bed of blue and gold flowers from the rocks, and a stepping-stone path connected the flowering bank with the mound.

Anxious, Lin rushed forward again. Jake lunged to stop her, but she eluded his grasp. As she cleared the blanket of flowers, a sand-colored snake with a red crescent on its head struck out, missing its mark. Squealing, Lin jumped back, turned, and ran. The reptile slithered away into the swirling sand.

Jake stared at the spectacle. Thousands of sand-colored snakes wiggled over and under the desert floor. He glanced at the stepping stones. The rocks were not level with the terrain, but rose three feet into the air. Nog must have used them to cross to the mound in hopes of getting the gold ball. Looking up, Jake did not see the huge viper that had bitten Nog, but he knew it was there, camouflaged in the rock.

Like the canyon mesa, the mound was set off from the main route. If Nog had just kept walking, he would have stayed safe. Jake could not ignore the dangerous detour, either, but for different reasons. Nog had been lured into the trap by the gold ball and greed. Jake had to rescue Nog.

Easier said than done, Jake realized when he called Nog's name. The snake's head rose from the rocks above

Nog. The Ferengi boy's only response was a slight flick of his finger. Dr. Bashir had neutralized the poison, and Nog was conscious. But he was afraid to move because the giant viper continued to attack, preventing his escape. Somehow, Jake had to neutralize the snake.

Jake glanced back at Lin and Rotor and blinked in surprise. The Selay boy was lying in the sand by the edge of the flower bed, and Lin was kneeling beside him. "What happened?" he yelled.

"I don't know, Jake. He just collapsed."

Jake glanced at the sand-snakes, tracking their movements as they skimmed through the sand. None of them crossed the line between the sand and the flowers. He shouted to the Bajoran girl. "Move him away from the flowers! Far away!"

While Lin dragged Rotor clear, Jake picked a bunch of blue and gold blooms. Squatting, he held them over the sand. The ridges formed by the reptiles suddenly radiated outward, away from the flowers. He looked back at his friends.

Lin had managed to pull Rotor a good distance away, and the Selay was slowly coming around. Rotor sat up, shook his head, and gripped his midsection. The flowers made the reptilian boy sick.

Jake picked as many flowers as he could hold in two hands and raced to the stones. However, crossing to the mound was not going to be as easy as he had thought, either. There was barely enough room for one foot on each narrow top. The stones were also spaced about three feet apart, the length of Jake's stride.

Clutching the flowers, Jake spread his arms for balance and mounted the first step. Wobbling, he quickly placed his other foot on the next step. Arms flailing to keep from falling, he knew that any hesitation would send him sprawling into the wiggling mass of sand-snakes. He sprinted, leaping with one foot, then the next. It was an exercise in blind faith as much as athletic ability. One of the stones might be loose. One of the gaps might be too wide. A single slip could end it all. Jake jumped from stone to stone, trusting that the Zhodran programmers believed in fair play. At last, he planted both feet on solid ground. Safe.

Above him, Nog opened his eyes, but he did not speak or make any sudden moves that might provoke the viper hiding in the rock. Neither did Jake. He gave Nog a silent thumbs-up. Still gripping the flowers, Jake climbed quietly upward.

Then, at the top, Jake forgot all about Nog. Nothing could bring his mother back, but he had other, more realistic desires. Jake saw what he wanted most in life. He did not see a gold ball, the symbol of wealth that no Ferengi could resist. Jake saw Earth. Wisps of white cloud encircled a brown-patched, blue globe spinning in the rocky depression. The promise of an impossible dream beckoned. If Jake had the globe, he could go to Earth.

"Jake," Nog hissed through clenched teeth.

Jake ignored him. Earth called, a whisper in his mind. Dropping the flowers, Jake reached for the blue ball. His father had promised to take him to Earth to live. They had come to Deep Space Nine instead. Jake had agreed to give the station a chance, partly because of Nog, but

mostly because Benjamin Sisko wanted to stay. Deep in his heart, Jake still wanted Earth. No matter what, no matter how selfish, that was all he really wanted—

Jake snatched his hand back and quickly gathered up the flowers. The viper was coiled six inches from his foot. Venomous fangs gleamed in its open mouth. Poised to attack, the monstrous diamond-shaped head drew back as Jake shoved the flowers in its face. The reptile retreated a few feet, then stopped to wait.

Nog blinked and sat up. "How'd you do that?"

Trembling, Jake stared at the snake. He had come within a split second of disaster and needed a moment to catch his breath. Selfish greed had almost cost him the game . . . and his life.

Nog, never missing a profitable opportunity, turned to get the gold ball. It was so heavy, he needed both hands to lift it.

"Put it down, Nog," Jake ordered breathlessly.

"No! It's worth a fortune!"

"It's not worth anything if you're stuck on this rock." Jake nodded toward the viper sliding into position above Nog. Below, the sand-snakes were wiggling and swarming around the raised stone steps. Nog could not jump the steps holding the heavy gold ball. He needed his hands for flowers and balance.

Nog hesitated. The viper's mouth opened. Dropping the ball, Nog took the flowers Jake offered, but he was incensed. "What's the point of playing this game if there's no way to win?"

Jake shrugged. Nog didn't need to know he had struck a bad bargain with Bokat when he had agreed to play.

There was no profit in the venture. The only way to win the Zhodran Crystal Quest was to survive it.

Jake did not look back as he scrambled down the mound. He'd get to Earth someday—on his own. For now he was happy that he and his father were together. Where they lived wasn't important.

Back on the main path, Jake took the lead again. Nog shuffled beside him, sulking over the loss of his riches. Tena Lin and Rotor trudged behind in grim silence. The sun was sinking toward the horizon, and as the terrain slowly changed from desert to marsh, Jake was stricken with an ominous dread.

Daylight dimmed as the trail drove into a swamp. Gnarled trees covered with tangled brown vines closed in around them. Broad, slimy leaves floated on stagnant water on either side of the narrow walkway. Thick curtains of moss hung from dead tree branches over the path, slowing their progress. The hoots and howls of creatures hidden in the shadows chilled the blood and warned of greater danger ahead. Total darkness would soon envelop them. Was he running out of time?

The road through the swamp got steadily harder to follow. Trailing vines snagged at Jake's arms. Knotted tree roots erupted from the soggy ground to trip him. A heavy mist formed over still gray waters as the remaining light waned and the air cooled. Desperate and uncertain, Jake led his friends deeper into a darkening gloom that seemed to go forever.

Exhausted, Jake stumbled and fell into a tangle of vines suspended over the murky water. He cried out as

heavy organic ropes twisted around him. He tried to rip the vines away, but the harder he fought, the stronger the net became. The choking vines drew him down toward the water.

"Jake!" Nog stopped dead, too petrified to help. Tena Lin grabbed for Jake's outstretched hand, but she couldn't reach it.

The vines tightened and dragged Jake closer to deadly swamp waters that weren't even real, except in his mind. Worse. Dr. Bashir would continue to revive him. He wouldn't die. He would drown over and over again through all eternity.

Cold water seeped through the back of his jumpsuit. Jake stiffened, then tensed as water washed over his face. The vines plunged him deeper into the dirty swamp.

Inspiration struck suddenly. Submerged and unable to breathe, Jake forced himself to relax. The organic mesh loosened slightly. This was a devious game, but it had rules. He was not a helpless victim of the alien device. His own panic was killing him. He had to achieve a state of total calm and hope he did not black out from lack of oxygen before the vines surrendered.

Relax, Jake. The crushing net eased, but Jake was wary of reacting too soon even though his lungs screamed for air. *Not yet . . .* Cautiously he moved an arm, then the other arm and his legs. And he was free. Out of breath, but afraid the deadly vines would snag him again, Jake slowly pushed upward. Stay calm . . . His head broke the surface of the water. Gasping for air, Jake crawled up the bank to the path and collapsed to collect his thoughts.

Blind luck combined with rational thinking had gotten him through the alien game so far. Now he knew why.

CHAPTER 12

"What happened?" Nog looked at Jake anxiously. "I thought we'd lost you for sure."

"I think I just got an A in panic control." Getting to his feet, Jake grinned at his confused companions. They weren't home yet, but their chances had greatly improved. "The end isn't too far now, and I want to get going." Turning, he marched boldly into the dark swamp.

Keeping a watchful eye out for any other hidden dangers, Jake reviewed his theory. Every game had a point and pushed the limits of a player's abilities. This program altered the specifics of each scenario according to the player. The Ferengi Bokat had called the game the Zhodran Crystal Quest. According to Dax, the Zhodran called the device the Crown of Ultimate Wisdom.

"I wish I'd never heard of this stupid game," Nog muttered.

"It's not a game," Jake said. "It's a test."

"A test!" All three children shouted in unison.

Nog's face reddened with indignation. "That's impossible. There's no profit in a test!"

"A test for what?" Lin asked.

"Character." Jake immediately regretted his honest response. Tena Lin and Rotor glared at him.

Nog sagged in humiliation. "I've been had! Conned into taking a dumb test with no reward! This is the worst deal I've made in my life!"

Jake decided not to explain in detail. The Zhodran wouldn't give him extra points for making his friends feel worse. Tena Lin had seen a Cardassian guarding the dock. Jake had seen a Borg. Both had been confronted with the thing they feared most in the universe—a test of courage Lin had failed. Also, Jake had not killed the Borg, which demonstrated compassion and a respect for all life. He wasn't sure what he had proved by goading Tena Lin into following him up the cliff—loyalty, understanding, leadership? Perhaps it didn't matter. While Rotor had acted foolishly when baited by the Antican, Jake had refused to fight Tommy Watson for stupid reasons. Lured by the gold ball, Nog had succumbed to greed and selfishness. Jake had chosen Nog's life over Earth—his heart's fondest desire.

"I don't get it." Rotor shook his head. "There must be a purpose to such an elaborate deception. Someone stands to gain *something.*"

Nog brightened. "He's right, Jake. There must be a prize for passing the test!"

Jake could only guess at the reasons for such a dangerous test, but again he kept silent.

The game left no margin for faking one's real personality or character. Dax had said the Zhodran were afraid of outsiders. Maybe they used the device to learn about each new species they encountered. If so, it meant the Zhodran were unwilling to invest the time and take the risk of getting to know people socially. Members of the Federation gradually developed understanding through personal contact and experience. Jake didn't approve of the Zhodran method, but like it or not, he was being tested as a representative of the human race. If he failed, all humans lost, and he would forfeit his mind. So far, Jake had succeeded on his own merit, but knowing it was a test made the pressure worse.

He still had to pass the final exam—the test of Ultimate Wisdom.

The terrain changed, suddenly and dramatically. The swamp was left behind as the path wound into another forest. White wildflowers and bushes with red and blue berries flourished among leafy, green trees. Although the sun had set, the light of three moons and a brilliant cluster of stars illuminated the woods. A warm yellow glow shown from a clearing ahead.

The end of the game.

Emerging from the trees, Jake paused to stare at a huge set of doors set into the face of another cliff. Small crystals embedded in the rock twinkled with reflected starlight. The glow came from a crystal mosaic inlaid in the doors. A huge padlock ran through two large handles, sealing the barrier.

Tena Lin gasped in awe. "It's so beautiful! The prize must be behind those doors!"

"Do you have any idea what it might be, Jake?" Nog prodded.

"The secret location of the Da-hahn Crystal," Jake said softly. "If the legend is true."

"The Da-hahn Crystal! That's got a priority-one rating on the Ferengi list of missing artifacts!" Nog rubbed his hands in greedy delight, excited by the prospect of unlimited wealth.

"What's the Da-hahn Crystal?" Rotor shivered with anticipation, his scales glistening in the moonlight.

Nog was quick to answer. "A treasure beyond my wildest dreams! It's the key to immortality! Whoever owns it is invincible!" He sank to his knees and raised his fists toward the stars. "I will rule the Ferengi Empire!"

"Power beyond imagination!" Rotor cried. "The Anticans could not stand against the Selay if we possessed that crystal. Victory at long last!"

"Bajor could make the Cardassians pay for the crimes they committed against us!" Lin snarled. "Their empire will be ours!"

Jake listened, but said nothing. The decision he made now would determine their fates. He could not make a mistake. As his companions bolted for the door, he lingered behind to think.

Rotor pounded on the massive barrier. "Open up! In the name of my father, Gaynor, Captain of the Selay ship *Erlan,* I command you!"

Taking a less violent approach, Tena Lin carefully felt along the seams, looking for a hidden control panel.

Nog jiggled the handles, but the sturdy padlock held. "There must be a key here somewhere!" Frantic, Nog began to search.

"I have the key." Jake casually strolled forward.

"Where?" Rotor hissed menacingly. "Give it to me."

"I can't." Sighing, Jake met Rotor's demanding gaze. "I'm the one connected to the Zhodran device back in the Infirmary. I have to solve this problem. You're all just spectators."

"We'll rule the Ferengi Empire together!" Nog clamped his arm around Jake's shoulders. "You are my best friend, right?"

Rotor rattled, and Lin bristled.

"Yes, I'm your best friend, Nog. And I'm going to try to get you out of here alive. All of you." He looked at Lin and Rotor intently. "There's nothing you can do to help, understand? Only my decisions can affect the device."

All three hesitated, then nodded.

"Okay. I hope this works," Jake muttered softly as he faced the door. Clasping his hands in front of him, he just stood there. A minute passed, two minutes, then five. Jake waited, ignoring the restless shuffling and discontented murmurs from the three observers behind him. While they had been attacking the door, Jake had decided that one of the character traits a fearful species like the Zhodran would value was patience. If he was wrong, they could be standing here for a very long time.

Five minutes became ten. Twice Nog opened his mouth to comment, then changed his mind. Rotor's tongue flicked in and out impatiently. Lin scowled at the ground, tapping her foot. Jake stood perfectly still,

waiting. Fifteen minutes. He heard a click, then smiled. With trembling hands he reached for the lock. A quick tug and the U-shaped steel bar separated from the rounded bottom portion. A twist, and the quaint device slipped from the handles. Jake put his hand on the door, then hesitated.

"What are you waiting for?" Disbelief flashed in Nog's eyes. "Open it, Jake."

Rotor couldn't stand the tension. He rushed forward and threw himself at the door. The massive door didn't budge, and he bounced off to land with a thud on the ground.

"Come on, Jake." Nog shook Jake's arm. "Everything you could possibly want will be yours! Wealth. Power . . ."

Jake shook his head slowly and removed his hand.

"Oh, great!" Lin spit fire. "The most powerful weapon in the universe is sitting there, waiting for someone to claim it, and Jake won't open the door!"

Ignoring the taunts and pleas, Jake stepped back. Being invincible and immortal wouldn't be any fun at all. A sense of accomplishment depended on overcoming obstacles—against the odds, with no guarantees, despite pain and hardship. There would be no challenge, no thrill, if winning was easy and assured. And life was sweeter because it didn't last forever.

The Zhodran called the device the Crown of Ultimate Wisdom. If there really was a Da-hahn Crystal, it was too powerful for anyone to own. The wisest thing to do was walk away.

And Jake did.

With his friends still trying to convince him to open the door, Jake turned his back on it and awakened in the Infirmary.

"Jake?" His father gasped and grabbed his hand. Dark eyes filled with tears of relief. "Welcome back, son."

Jake blinked, confused for a moment. "Did I pass the test?"

Sisko smiled. "With flying colors."

"This is not possible!" A tall, thin, white-haired alien dressed in blue stepped to the foot of the biobed. He held a silver rod that sparkled with blue light and hummed. "No one has ever returned. Not in two thousand years!"

"There's a first time for everything." Dr. Bashir lifted the device off Jake's head. He handed it to Sisko, then looked at the alien with a smug, satisfied grin.

The amazed alien stared at Jake. *Must be a Zhodran,* Jake thought. Fighting a slight dizziness, he sat up and watched as Dax removed the Federation helmets from the other three children. They all seemed a bit dazed, too, but they had made it back with him. Lin and Rotor ran off as soon as Dr. Bashir gave them permission. Nog waited, still hoping for a profitable miracle.

"But he's just a child!" the alien exclaimed.

"No, Talarn. He's not a child." Sisko beamed with pride and clasped Jake's shoulder. "Not anymore."

Jake grinned, too choked with emotion to say anything.

"No one? In two thousand years?" Swinging his legs over the side of the biobed, Nog leered at the stunned Zhodran. "Jake saved our lives and beat your game. There must be some reward."

Jake punched Nog in the arm. "We're alive. Isn't that enough?"

Nog glared at Jake. "Not for a Ferengi."

"I'm not a Ferengi."

"No, you're not. You're quite human, Jake." Dr. Bashir scanned Jake with the medical tricorder. "And none the worse for wear after your ordeal."

"Actually, it was kinda fun." Jake sighed wistfully. "Zhodran is a beautiful planet. It reminded me of Earth."

O'Brien gathered up the Federation helmets and

winked at Jake. "You might be able to visit Zhodran soon."

Talarn's blazing blue eyes widened. "No one visits Zhodran."

"But Jake passed the test." Dr. Bashir focused his pointed gaze on the Zhodran.

Sisko nodded with a serious expression, hiding a smile. "And as a representative of the Federation, he's earned us the right to open diplomatic relations and trade negotiations with your world."

The Zhodran's mouth fell open.

"Your rules, Talarn," O'Brien said. "Not ours."

Talarn's shoulders sagged in defeat. Then he smiled. "My government will contact you as soon as I return home with this remarkable news. But we will only meet with a *human* ambassador from the Federation. No other species will be permitted."

"I'm certain that can be arranged. And perhaps, in the future, others will be welcome, too." Sisko gave the Zhodran crown back to Talarn. "As I promised."

Talarn bowed. "The father is as honorable as the son." Tucking the alien device under his white fur cloak, the Zhodran priest glided majestically out the door.

Pleased, Jake looked at Nog. The young Ferengi gazed at him with renewed awe and respect. Not only had Jake won the game and saved his friends, he had single-handedly paved the way for Federation trade with a whole new market. Of course, Nog would soon scorn him again—once he found out that Jake would not profit from the deal personally. Sometimes there was just no way to win.

"Commander!" Quark raced into the Infirmary. He

halted before Sisko with a causal glance at Nog. "Glad to see you're back among the conscious, Nog. Your shift starts in an hour."

Nog shrugged and rolled his eyes, but inside, he was delighted. The curt exchange had been rather emotional for Ferengi. Quark was relieved and happy that Nog was okay.

"What can I do for you, Quark?" Sisko was not amused.

"When you've got a moment, I'd like to talk to you about leasing the Games Bazaar. At least, while Bokat is in jail." Quark slumped into a begging posture. "The arcade provides harmless entertainment. It keeps the children busy and out of trouble." He scowled at Nog. "Most of them anyway."

"Aside from the thousands of credits the business earns every day," Dax added with a twinkling smile.

"Profit goes without saying," Quark countered.

"I'll think about it." Dismissing Quark, Sisko turned back to Jake. "Are you sure you're feeling all right?"

"I feel great." Jumping off the biobed, Jake grabbed Nog and headed for the door. "But I've still got to finish that paper on the Crusades." He bolted down the Promenade before his father could comment, dragging Nog behind him. Once they were clear of the Infirmary, Nog dug in his heels, refusing to go any farther.

"I've got better things to do than watch you write a report for school! We need a marketing plan for Zhodran!"

"We don't have anything to sell on Zhodran, Nog." They were always at odds over their different value systems, and Jake was desperate to preserve some of

Nog's respect. However, he couldn't lie about their prospects concerning Zhodran. "That's why I've got to finish this paper."

Nog eyed Jake suspiciously. "There's profit in it?"

"Maybe," Jake hedged. He now realized that valuable lessons could be learned from the past. Tena Lin, Rotor, and Nog had made mistakes in the Zhodran game. Knowing what *not* to do had helped Jake win. History might come in very handy someday—for both of them. But since Nog wouldn't understand any motive that was not clearly and immediately profitable, some Ferengi strategy was required. "Quark wants to acquire the Games Bazaar because business is good, but eventually people are going to get bored playing the same games over and over again, right?"

Nog nodded thoughtfully. "That seems logical."

"So, I figure, since I've put all this effort into learning about the Crusades, I might as well make money from it."

"How?" Despite his reservations, the chance of financial gain aroused Nog's curiosity.

Jake steered him toward the nearest crossover bridge. "We can invent our own game and sell it to Quark! In the Crusades, kings and knights traveled to a distant, dangerous land on a quest. They rode horses and fought a war against fierce desert tribes with swords and shields. It's perfect! For a game."

Nodding, Nog chuckled with enthusiasm. "I'll make a decent Ferengi out of you yet, hew-mon." Then the questions started flying. "What's a horse? Why were they fighting? Was there profit in the war? Who won?"

"That's what we're going to find out." Jake grinned as he keyed for the turbolift. Knowledge was the real key to success. If Jake had to play by Ferengi rules to help Nog learn, then so be it. After all, Jake was human. He never gave up, and nothing was impossible—not even an educated Ferengi.

About the Author

DIANA G. GALLAGHER lives in California with her daughter, Chelsea; her best friend, Betsey; three dogs, and five cats. Her grown son, Jay, lives in Kansas. When she's not writing, she likes to read, work in the garden, and walk the dogs. A Hugo award–winning illustrator, she is best known for her series *Woof: The House Dragon.* Her songs about humanity's future in space are sung at science fiction conventions throughout the world and have been recorded in cassette form: *Cosmic Concepts More Complete, Star*Song,* and *Fire Dream.* Her first novel, *The Alien Dark,* appeared in 1990.

About the Illustrator

TODD CAMERON HAMILTON is a self-taught artist who has resided all his life in Chicago, Illinois. He has been a professional illustrator for the past ten years, specializing in fantasy, science fiction, and horror. Todd is the current president of the Association of Science Fiction and Fantasy Artists. His original works grace many private and corporate collections. He has co-authored two novels and several short stories. When not drawing, painting, or writing, his interests include metalsmithing, puppetry, and teaching.